AVA GREENE

The Origins of the Sea

JARED
SAIS

Disclaimer — This is a work of fiction. Character names and descriptions are the product of the author's imagination. Any resemblance to actual persons, living or dead, is entirely coincidental.

Cover art: Brandon Dorman
Formatting: CreativeBlueprintDesign.com

ISBN 979-8-218-14553-8 (Paperback)
Printed in the United States of America
Published by Sais Publishing
www.saispublishing.com

Dedication

My dear mother, you have been the only person to read this book more than I have. Words cannot express the depth of my gratitude for your endless love and unwavering care. I humbly dedicate Ava Greene to you, as a small token of my appreciation and a testament to your immense impact on my life. A dream within a dream.

Special Thank You

Thank you to all my students who have inspired me beyond words. Your unwavering passion for learning and curiosity have motivated me to put pen to paper. As a token of my gratitude, your names will forever be etched in these pages.

To Avi,

You make me so proud, my son. Your smile lights up the room and gives me such joy. Never give up on your dreams and always know that I am right by your side, cheering you on.

Never allow anyone to discourage you by saying "you can't." Their limitations do not define your potential. If you hold a dream close to your heart, it is already a reality waiting to unfold. Believe in yourself, always.

Love, Dad

My Dearest Hilary,

I find it difficult to put into words the depth of my gratitude for the love and unwavering support you have given me throughout the many years. You are not only the love of my life but also the shining beacon that illuminates our family's path.

Forever our queen.

Love, Jared

Table of Contents

1

Glory

Nothing much ever happened in the town of Noblesville, Indiana. That is, until that one day—which happened to be the day of Noblesville High's big swim meet.

Ava Greene loved her cozy house, her welcoming street, her sleepy neighborhood full of exceedingly polite, friendly people. But on this particular morning, although everything looked the same, she couldn't shake the feeling that something was off.

Ava thought it was just nerves as she donned a long-sleeved jacket before stepping outside to make her way to school. Though it was early summer, there was a crispness in the air that made her shiver slightly. Closing the front door behind her, she turned around to take in the picturesque scene of multi-colored flowers resting in brown mulch. The chilly breeze caused a handful of leaves to float down from a nearby tree and swirl in midair. Her block came to life just as the sun began to shine and warm her fair skin. She brushed her wind-blown golden-brown hair off of her face. With her eyes closed, she smiled as the day rose to greet her.

"Good morning, Ava."

This wasn't Mother Nature, however. It was a male voice, calling out from a car idling in the driveway.

"Earth to Ava!" Kevin shouted, his tousled brown locks, streaked with auburn, blowing in the breeze. It looked like sandy finger-waves on a beach after the tide had receded. "Kevin!" she exclaimed, beaming at him.

"Hope you're ready for today," he said as she approached his car. "You only have the entire school counting on you."

Ava grimaced as she slid into the front passenger seat, the familiar nerves dancing in her stomach. "No pressure or anything!" As Kevin drove to school, he turned down the radio and said, "So, kind of a big day. I mean, besides the whole championship thing."

Ava looked over at him, baffled. This last, all-important swim meet of the season was all she'd been able to think about for weeks. "Big day?"

"Um, it's your birthday? June nineteenth?" Kevin said, giving her a confused look. "Today is the nineteenth, isn't it?"

"Oh, yeah. I guess it is!" She shook her head in disbelief. How could she have forgotten her own Sweet Sixteen?

"Well then. Happy birthday, happy last week of school, and soon . . . happy championship win." Kevin smiled.

Ava forced a grin despite her nerves and tried to enjoy the warm summer breeze, blowing through her hair. Now that Kevin had his license, she loved when he had the mornings free from baseball practice to take her to school, in his sweet Wrangler with the top down. She loved pulling up to the parking lot in his Jeep after years of taking the bus. It felt like freedom. Usually. Today, she had other things on her mind.

"And today is a half day!" Kevin added. "So, we can celebrate after the big win."

Her stomach churned. *Win. Way to put the cart way ahead of the horse, Kev.* "Yikes. I can't believe the entire town took the afternoon off to see the championship. I mean, what if I lose?"

"You're not going to lose."

"But what if I do?" Her question came out as a whine, and she hated it. She wanted to be confident. She *needed* to be.

"Just do the best you can today, Ava." Kevin took her hand. "I'm already proud of you."

The warmth of Kevin's touch briefly washed away Ava's anxiety but, as they pulled into the school parking lot, she felt the worry creeping back onto her face. That was one of the problems of growing up in Small Town, USA. Without much else going on, all eyes were on the star athletes. Not only was the school counting on their star swimmer to win, but the entire town expected it.

Anxiety rushed throughout her body as he pulled into his space in the lot.

Her pounding heart beat courage into her like how drums on a battlefield moved an army towards victory, or defeat. As Ava entered the building, she spotted a garish new gold-and-purple banner that read, "GO, PIRANHAS, GO!!!" hanging above a case teeming with trophies, gold medals, and first place ribbons.

Ava froze. Kevin put his arm around her and leaned in, likely to say something inspiring or comforting, but the bell for first period clanged over their heads. Kevin looked up at it and instead blurted, "Smells like pizza for lunch!"

Ava turned to him, her confusion giving way to a grin. "Was that your way of trying to calm me down?"

Kevin shrugged sheepishly.

Ava laughed and gave him a playful punch. "Well, it worked."

Ava took her assigned seat, trying hard to ignore the glances and whispers from her fellow students. The few times Ava looked up, she smiled politely and nodded but, in truth, as the minutes ticked by, the attention made her feel more and more sick to her stomach. As Mr.

Samson positioned himself at the front of the classroom, the students' eyes finally moved away from Ava. She breathed a sigh of relief.

"Good morning, class. I'm sure you all did your homework," Mr. Sampson said in a deep voice that revealed equal parts of hope and sarcasm.

Nervous laughter filled the classroom. It was the last week of school, and most of the kids' heads were filled with dreams of summer vacation, not meaningless busy work.

Mr. Samson chuckled. "As many of you know, we have a proud tradition here at Noblesville High. For the past four years, our swimming program has ranked among the best in the nation. This year, it is second in the nation, thanks to a certain someone . . ." He grinned proudly at Ava. "I am confident our star swimmer, Ava Greene, will lead us to victory once again in our State Championship, and I couldn't be prouder."

Mr. Samson's words pierced Ava's lungs like daggers, and for a moment she stopped breathing. He must have noticed, because his tone quickly changed. "We will all be there to support you, win or lose, Ava. Now, since there's no hope of getting any of you to focus this week, let's watch a movie."

The students cheered as the lights went off, and in the darkness, Ava found her breath again. As the movie began, Ava stared out the window at birds, gliding through the sky. She imagined herself as one of them—flying away, no responsibilities, no medals, no one counting on her.

The lights flashed back on when the bell rang, jolting Ava out of her reverie. Her chest tightened again.

"Okay, class, have a wonderful day! Don't cause too much trouble," Mr. Samson called after them.

As Ava walked through the hallways, students cheered and stuck their hands into her path for high-fives.

Lunch came after second period. Ava wolfed down her pizza in order to make a speedy exit and avoid the juiced-up atmosphere of the cafeteria. Only one more class to get through before the end of the shortened day. And then it would be time for the swim meet.

This was her favorite class—AP European History. Ava quickened her pace as she entered the room, gliding to her seat, eyes glued to the door. As Kevin entered the room and met her gaze, her chest burst with warmth.

Kevin sat beside her and whispered, "It's going to be okay."

As nice as it was that he knew everything she was thinking, without having to say a word, her gut still twisted.

"And what if it's not? What if I lose?"

"That's what binge-eating birthday cake is for."

Ms. Page adjusted the purple rimmed glasses on her thin nose and cleared her throat. The sound was loud enough to instantly get the attention of the chattering class.

"Unlike many of your other teachers, I will be leading a normal class today and for the rest of the week," Ms. Page declared. "Take out your books and we'll begin."

The class groaned.

As Ava opened her notebook, her throat began to feel dry and scratchy. She swallowed, but she couldn't seem to get any saliva going to moisten it.

She was thirsty. She licked her lips, trying to decide if it was actual thirst, boredom, anxiety, or all three.

It didn't matter. Within the next few moments, she began to feel like she was surrounded by desert on all sides. Her throat was like sandpaper. She felt like she might shrivel up and die without water.

She raised her hand. "Excuse me, Ms. Page? May I get a drink of—"

"Not now, Miss Greene, class has just begun," Ms. Page snapped before she could finish.

Ava tried to focus on her notetaking, but she couldn't shake the feeling that something was off. Her throat was growing scratchy and sore each time she swallowed, like it was drying out by the second. Her tongue felt hard and thick. She began playing with her hair to distract herself. As she twirled a strand through her fingers, she noticed a streak of shiny bluish-purple.

"Kevin, look at my hair," Ava whispered.

"Did you get ink in it?"

Ava looked down at her fountain pen. "I must have."

"Quiet down, over there," Ms. Page shot in their direction.

Knees bounced and pens tapped on desks with increasing restlessness as the moments dragged on. Though Ms. Page was their strictest teacher, even she looked at the clock as if counting down the minutes. Ava couldn't stop looking at her hair, and kept swallowing, trying to moisten her desert-dry mouth.

Finally, class ended. Time to move on.

"See you all at the Natatorium," Ms. Page called over the bell.

Ava was the first one out the door. She had two missions now: first, drink a gallon of water; then, win the race.

She couldn't tell if her speed had to do with her need to get the race over with, or her excitement at the prospect of being back in the water. Ava felt at home there. It was the closest thing she could imagine to how those birds must feel.

Ava stopped at the water fountain and greedily gulped water. Then she grabbed her swim bag out of her locker and rushed to the school bus waiting outside. She was met with a wave of cheers from her teammates as she climbed onto the bus.

She couldn't help but smile as she sat down next to a tall, blonde girl named Ashley Penzal.

"Hey, birthday girl!" Ashley shouted, giving her a hug.

"Thanks, Ash. I'm too nervous to even think right now. My brain is hyper-focused on the meet," Ava mumbled.

Ashley's hazel eyes glinted in the sunlight. "Well, let's win this thing today so you can really celebrate." The bus set off for the pool, and the closer the girls got to their destination, the more their excitement seemed to rise, until it was at a fever pitch. As the bus pulled into the parking lot, they screamed their final cheer in unison: "I know, I know, we know, we know, they know, they know, that we . . . will . . . win!" The girls stomped their feet and slapped the backs of the bus seats.

Even their short, fiery coach, Carmela Dean, and Mr. Johnson, the portly bus driver, joined in. The proud coach clapped forcefully, and the driver honked his horn to punctuate the chant.

The only person who wasn't cheering was Ava. She stared out the window, thinking about the meet, doing a mental check of every muscle to make sure she was feeling in tip-top condition.

She could do this. Everyone believed in her. Kevin believed in her.

And if it didn't happen, so what? It was just like he said—they could go home and drown their sorrows with birthday cake. It would be fine.

With that, her anxiety gave way to excitement. When the bus stopped, she put her game face on, hopped from her seat, and walked confidently to the front of the bus. Ava led the way through the open door and into the pool complex.

Once inside the locker rooms, the girls quietly changed into their swim gear, and then sat on the benches awaiting their coach's "attack plan."

Coach Dean detailed her strategy. For the 400 Freestyle, Noblesville would be facing off against a competing school's star swimmer—a girl named Natalie Turrell, who was well regarded as one of the top swimmers in the state. Coach Dean finished by saying, "Don't worry, girls. We have our secret weapon."

The other girls nodded, and Ava felt another gut punch. She forced a smile.

Coach Dean continued, "Today, the only team that stands in our way to the state championship is the Indianapolis Panthers.

I don't have to remind you of the hard work we've done to get to this point. But it's not over yet. You will have to push—and when you feel like stopping, you will push forward. When you feel like you can't swim any farther, you will keep going! When your body feels like it's about to fall apart and your lungs are on fire, you . . . *will* . . . swim . . . faster! That is what giving one hundred percent feels like!"

Ava saw the excitement radiating from Coach Dean's face. She studied the faces of her teammates. They would make her proud or die trying.

"Together we will smash through obstacles, fly past the competition, and win our glory. Glory!" Coach Dean bellowed, with her fists clenched victoriously above her head and her round face as red as a tomato.

Ava clapped her hands, ready for battle. In their team huddle, Coach Dean gave one last cry, and the girls screamed right along with her: "Glory on three! One, two, three, glory!"

The announcer's megaphone and the crowd's cheers wafted through the locker room doors.

"Sounds like they're ready for us," a calmer Coach Dean prompted.

The girls followed her through the doors toward the swimming hall. Ava stayed back a moment to clear her head. After taking a couple of deep breaths, she stood up and walked slowly to the door. People were starting to chant her name. Her mother and Kevin would be out there in the throng somewhere. They loved her, supported her, no matter what.

In that moment, all her nervousness dissipated. She felt it, thrumming in her veins. She couldn't wait to be in the water.

She was made for this.

As the team passed through the swinging doors, the crowd started to roar, and the band played. Chants of "Go Piranhas, Go!" and "Let's go, Panthers!" filled the hall.

No matter how many times Ava swam in this pool, she would never get over just how beautiful it was. The Olympic-sized pool, with its banner-covered walls and white-tiled floor, was a spiritual place to her. White beams crisscrossed the ceiling, forming an intricate design that reminded her of the architecture of King's Cross station in London. Ava looked up at her school flag. The gold and purple pennant hung above her team, infusing her with school pride. She still couldn't believe they had gotten this far.

As she reached the bench, Coach Dean pulled her aside.

"Ava, how do you feel?"

Far from the swagger of her locker room speech, Coach Dean's words sounded slightly panicked.

"Good," she replied confidently, giving her a double-thumbs-up. "I'm ready."

Her coach patted her back. "Good. Now go out there and do what you always do."

She still had time until her event, so Ava sat on the bench and cheered on her teammates, timing her loudest cheers for when her teammates emerged from the water to take their breaths.

As she was watching the four-by-100-meter individual medley, she glanced over at the Panthers bench and noticed a girl shooting a death stare back at her.

Ava had encountered many competitive girls over the years, but the stare across the pool looked different. She didn't quite seem cocky, but rather as if Ava had done something to personally offend her. The girl was just a bit taller than Ava, with long legs and arms, bright blue eyes, and strawberry blonde hair.

Natalie Turrell. It had to be.

Ava swallowed and tore her gaze away.

The buzzer signaled the end of the event, which the Piranhas won by a long shot. The two schools were now dead even. It would all come down to the last race—Ava's race.

Of course. Ava rose to her feet, her knees only slightly wobbly. *I can do this.*

The 400-meter Freestyle was the longest race of the day. As Ava walked toward the pool, she saw the girl with the deadly glare walking toward her, eyes transfixed on her.

"You're not much to look at, are you?" sneered Natalie when they were nearly toe-to-toe. Ava stood speechless, stunned.

After waiting a beat for a response, the girl just laughed bitterly and walked on to her starting position.

Regaining her composure, Ava got into her own position. *Depends on who's looking*, she thought. *Why, Ava, why? Why do you always think of witty comebacks two seconds after you need them?*

She crouched down and gathered herself into a coiled spring, drawing her attention away from her opponent. Like a cheetah ready to pounce on her prey, she focused on the water ahead, waiting for the signal.

Ava could smell the heavy scent of chlorine in the water. She felt her breath slow and her feet grip into the gritty starting block, ready to push off.

Then the buzzer sounded.

Like a lightning bolt, Ava dove into the water. Once submerged, she moved like a dolphin, pumping her legs and navigating the water with her hands pointed overhead. Popping back up above the surface, she began to alternate her strokes, gracefully gliding through the water. Her hands flattened parallel to her body to better cut through the water the way an oar would more freely navigate the tide when tilted on its side.

Her vigorous strokes advanced her to an early lead during the first 100-meters, but Natalie would not be outdone. By the 200-meter mark, they were almost head-to-head, with Ava in the lead by only a hand's length. They remained neck and neck until the 250-meter mark, when Natalie started to creep past Ava. Each set of strokes put a different girl ahead. Every time she surfaced, Ava could hear the crowd cheering wildly. Usually by now, Ava had a dominating lead over her competition, but this girl was still right beside her. Another stroke, and Ava was sure Natalie would pass her.

Ava's heartbeat pounded in her ears. *Faster, Ava. You must go faster.*

She pushed her muscles to the absolute limit, tasting that win. But at that moment, a sharp pain ran down her spine into her feet and hands.

She shook it off, pushing through the pain.

A cramp, that's all. Shake it off.

Mid-stroke, just as the pain began to subside, she noticed tiny bubbles, and what looked like microscopic organisms floating in the water.

That's weird, I think something's in my goggles, she thought fleetingly, trying not to lose focus. *Forget it. Keep moving.*

Time slowed. Ava caught a glimpse of her hand. It looked as though her fingers were webbed together and had acquired an unnatural, dark blue tint.

Horrified, she swallowed a gulp of water and began to choke. She had to come up for air.

As she emerged, sputtering, she looked frantically at her hand. It looked normal.

What is happening? she thought, looking to the side of the pool to see if anyone else had noticed.

The first thing she saw was Coach Dean, jumping up and down and pointing toward the end of the pool, screaming, "No! Not now! Swim Ava, swim!"

Ava caught her breath and managed a glance at her teammates while turning her head to take a breath. They stood in shocked silence, hands over their mouths.

Ava scanned the water for her opponent. Entering the final 100 meters, Natalie had a commanding lead and showed no sign of slowing down. She seemed so far away. It would take a miracle to catch her, now.

Ava thought about the moments before. All those people, depending on her for the victory. She couldn't give up now.

Ava took a deep breath, dove forward, and started to swim. Hard. Harder than she ever had in her life. With each powerful stroke, her heart raced, and an unbearable pain seared through her body, but this time she ignored it. She was too scared to look at her hands, so she kept her eyes closed as she surged toward the end of the race.

Ava stretched her body to its limit with each stroke, kicking her legs as hard as possible. All her thoughts were focused on winning as she plowed forward stroke after stroke after stroke. She didn't realize that she hadn't tilted her head to take a single breath. The thought of disappointing her town, Coach Dean, her mother, and Kevin made Ava push even harder. Each mighty stroke was matched by a jolting kick. As she entered the final turn into the last fifty meters, the pain grew stronger, sending shocks throughout her body. She refused to slow down.

With only one sprint left, the pain was all but gone. Ava sped up. Soon, she was soaring through the water. She lost all sense of her position in the race, and instead became focused on the gentle sensation of the water brushing by her skin like air . . . And then, abruptly, her hand touched the pool wall.

As she resurfaced, Ava felt as if she was emerging from a deep massage. She had never felt so relaxed, so weightless.

It took a second for her to realize that the cheering had faded. In fact, the pool hall was completely silent. There were no cheers or boos, not even screams from Coach Dean. In fact, everyone was frozen, like a photograph.

Looking at her.

Sure she must've been seeing things, Ava whipped off her goggles and confirmed it—a mixture of puzzled and incredulous faces stared back at her.

Oh, no, I lost.

But when Ava looked over into the other lane and didn't see the other girl's gloating face beside her, she spun in the water and realized that her opponent was still half a lap behind.

Ava had won.

Not just won but blown the other girl out of the water.

One of the judges began running toward Ava. As he reached the edge of the pool, he grasped her arm and yanked her out of the water.

After a quick examination, the judge looked back at the panel and shook his head.

What is going on? Do they think I cheated?

How fast could she possibly have been going? The judge looked at Ava one last time, shrugged, and lifted Ava's arm, announcing her as the victor.

The crowd erupted in cheers. Ava, still dazed, looked at her hand. It was utterly normal.

Stress. I was just seeing things because of stress, she assured herself as her teammates surrounded her, screaming "GLORY! GLORY!"

Ava hugged her teammates, trying to enjoy the moment.

But the thought still lurked in the back of her mind: *Something is very wrong.*

2

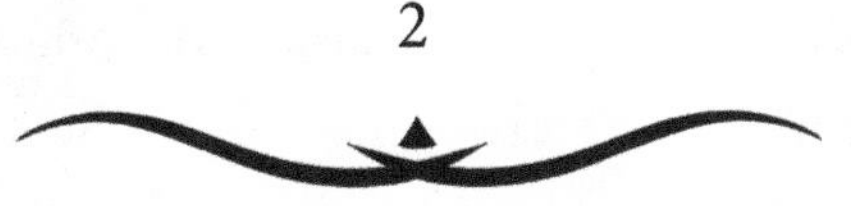

What's Happening to Me?

Ava sat alone in the empty locker room, rooted to the bench. The space had been full of energy and excitement before the race, but now it was as silent and cold as a tomb. Even the echoes of cheers had faded. Wild thoughts tumbled through Ava's mind as she thought back on the race. Microscopic organisms in the water, webbed hands, and that pain—the ruthless, unrelenting pain. And yet now, under the fluorescent lights of the locker room, everything seemed to be perfectly normal.

Am I going crazy, she wondered, staring at her perfectly normal hands. *And what about today, at school? I was so thirsty . . . and my hair, turning blue?*

She pulled out a strand of her hair, which was dry because of the swim cap. It was the normal dull beige color. Nothing to write home about.

And yet, all those things that had happened to her today . . .

What's happening to me?

As if on cue, Ava's phone rang and summoned her back to the real world.

"Hey, Kevin," she answered. She was trying to put the events of the race out of her mind, but even to herself, Ava sounded cold and distant.

"Ava! That was amazing! I'm waiting outside whenever you're ready. I told your mom we were going out, so she'll see you at home. We're both so proud of you, I can't wait to celebrate!"

"Okay, I'm on my way now." Robotically, Ava threw her jacket and sweatpants over her now-dry swimsuit, grabbed her bag, and quietly exited the complex. As she walked into the parking lot, she spotted Kevin's green Jeep. He was sitting in the front seat, rocking out to a song with a heavy bass line that mirrored the pounding of Ava's heart. When Kevin saw her, he quickly stopped dancing, lowered the music, and sat straight up in his seat as though he'd been like that the whole time.

Ava couldn't even bring herself to smile.

"I was hoping you wouldn't see that," he responded sheepishly, turning the key in the ignition and pulling out of the parking lot after she'd settled herself into the passenger seat.

"What?" she asked, only half-listening. If she was going crazy, Kevin would probably be the first to see it. Especially if she kept acting all in her head. She tried to shake off her fears and focused on him. "Oh, please, I've seen you do weirder things than that."

"So . . . speaking of weird things . . ." Kevin paused, and the silence that dragged on made Ava suddenly nervous.

"What?"

"What do you mean, what? Just now—your swimming? You, like, flew through the water! It was like you were . . . well, I guess, flying."

Ava's chest tightened. She had known there would be questions, but that didn't mean she was ready for them. What was she supposed to say? If she said she had seen her hands become webbed, Kevin would think she was delusional, but she didn't want to lie and say everything was normal, either. Ava felt the silence dragging on and knew she would have to say something, so she shrugged.

"I guess I just found my stroke," Ava finally managed, her words sounding brittle.

Kevin just stared at her, and Ava knew he wasn't buying it. "Ava, the way you swam, I mean—I've never seen anyone swim that fast! I don't think anyone ever has. You might seriously be the fastest swimmer in the world!"

The temperature in the cabin skyrocketed, and Ava flushed, desperate to change the subject. "Yeah. I guess I don't like to lose. Okay, I thought we were supposed to be celebrating. Where are we off to?"

Kevin's eyes lingered on her for a long moment, and the fear in Ava's heart didn't melt away until he cracked a small smile. "It's a surprise."

For Kevin's sake, Ava pasted on a smile and tried to look excited. But, in truth, right now, another surprise was the last thing she needed.

Kevin drove uphill on winding roads surrounded by swaths of towering pine trees. The view was mesmerizing. Ava couldn't help but be transfixed by it. She was so caught up in the blurry beauty, she was barely aware of anything else.

That is, until the view started to go backwards.

Ava snapped out of her reverie and looked over at Kevin, who was staring at the dashboard with panic in his eyes. The car had hit a hill so steep that it had stalled and just barely started to roll backwards.

He patted the dashboard and pushed a bit harder on the gas. "Don't worry, ol' Buffy can handle this. You know why I named her Buffy, right?"

"Because she's a mountain slayer," Ava said in a singsong voice, rolling her eyes playfully and repeating back the joke Kevin had told her so often.

"That's right!"

Even though Buffy had tackled many a hill in the months Ava had known her, she held on tight to the roof handle for a little extra reassurance as the car slowly climbed its way up the hill. "So, are you ready to tell me where we're going yet?"

"The question isn't where we're going, it's where we *are*," Kevin told her as he rounded the final turn.

The trees had cleared to reveal a stunning lake brimming with crystal clear water. Ava got out of the car and took a step toward the water, closing her eyes and just feeling the crisp, cool breeze as it brushed softly against her skin. The events of the race started to fade to the back of her mind, and she opened her eyes with fresh excitement about the moment she was sharing with the boy she loved.

Mountains formed a ring around the lake, their tree cover lusher than any she had seen before, and it created the feeling that she and Kevin had stepped into their own private paradise. The birds were singing so sweetly that she couldn't imagine a more perfect place to celebrate.

"It's beautiful!" Ava breathed, turning to face Kevin with wide, sparkling eyes. "How did you find this place?"

"I stumbled upon it one day when I was looking for new places to go hiking. Hidden to the world, but when I saw it, I thought it was made just for you." Kevin's words were endearing, and lifted Ava's soul with joy. "Happy birthday."

Ava ran into his arms to hug him, almost knocking the poor boy over. He chuckled and stumbled back a step before catching her, sliding his arms gently around her waist. The two stood peacefully, intertwined at the water's edge, listening to the waves lap at their feet. Ava shivered with happiness, enjoying the peace of the moment. After a long moment, Kevin pulled away with a warm smile.

"Want to go for a swim?"

"Do you even have to ask?"

Ava was still wearing her swimsuit from the competition, and she quickly stripped back down to it and tossed her clothes onto the beach. She looked at Kevin expectantly, ready to race into the water with him, only to find him staring at her with soft eyes.

"You're beautiful," he told her.

Ava's heart fluttered, but she didn't let that stop her from teasing Kevin the way she had for as long as she'd known him. "And you are a cornball."

"Can a cornball hold your hand?"

"Yes . . ."

"Can a cornball look into your eyes?"

Ava laughed, nodding her head as Kevin moved in closer.

"Can a cornball surprise you?"

"What—"

Before she had time to think, Kevin grabbed her around the waist, hoisted her up, and sprinted into the lake. She let out a shriek, more excited than scared, because she trusted him. His momentum combined with the added weight from carrying Ava shoved him so far forward that he tumbled sideways into the water, creating a giant splash that momentarily disrupted the serene environment. Even so, it was as if they were two hearts, in perfect sync. The two emerged from the water laughing and sputtering.

Ava and Kevin floated on their backs and stared up at the passing clouds, tossing back and forth opinions on what they looked like. Things got particularly heated when Kevin thought a cloud looked like a bunny, but Ava argued that it was clearly a dragon, and to make peace, Kevin stopped floating and pulled Ava gently into his arms. He gazed lovingly at her, using a tender hand to smooth her wet hair out of her face.

"Ava, these past two years with you have been amazing. How did a shy kid with a hoodie catch the captain of the swim team? I'll never know."

"What can I say, I saw your hotness even through your sweatshirt." She reached out to squeeze Kevin's hand, only to find that he was shivering violently. "Kev, you're freezing!"

"No, I'm okay—"

Ava straightened, panic setting in. His lips were blue, his teeth were chattering, and he couldn't keep his body from shaking with shivers. "We need to get you out of the water."

"You can warm me up!" he said, pulling her even closer. His arms wrapped tightly around her until they were close enough for their bodies to meld. "You're like an oven right now."

He wasn't kidding. His skin was icy to the touch, almost frozen. The air had become chillier as the sun went down and the lake hadn't exactly been warm to begin with. Ava wasn't really sure why she didn't feel cold herself. She set those thoughts aside and wiggled out of his grasp, though she didn't let go of his hand.

"We're going," Ava insisted as she started to pull him towards shore. "I can't have you freezing to death when we're still celebrating my birthday!"

The two ran back to the car and blasted the heat, changing out of their wet clothes as quickly as humanly possible. Kevin pressed his hands to the vents to try and warm his numb fingers and, when she saw his purple fingertips, Ava realized just how cold that water had been. A flash of panic shot through her once again.

What is going on?

She looked over at her shivering boyfriend. "Feeling better?"

"Much better, thank you." He tilted his head. "What's weird is that you're *not* freezing. That water must be fifty degrees."

He was right. She was usually *always* cold. She hated that feeling, too. But when she'd been in the water, she'd felt perfectly warm and content. Even more so than she did now.

Another weird thing. She shivered.

"Well, hey, if you're still cold, you could always do another dance for me," Ava teased.

Kevin took that as a challenge. He flailed and twisted in his seat, performing everything from the classic robot to vogue, that were so enthusiastic that Ava couldn't resist joining in. Despite the total lack of both space and music, the two rocked out so intensely that Ava's phone went flying off her seat and disappeared in the footwell of the car.

She felt beneath the seats in vain. "Kev, could you turn the light on? I'm trying to find my phone, but I can't see anything."

The light flicking on snapped them back into the real world. When Ava finally found her phone, it was buzzing with hundreds of notifications, people congratulating her on her swimming victory. Ava grimaced. The last thing she wanted was another reminder of today's championship and all the weirdness that had come from it. She just wanted to spend tonight thinking about Kevin.

"So, how does it feel to be a celebrity?" he said, before she could stuff the phone into her bag.

Ava sighed. "I don't think—"

"Woah, Ava, your eyes! What's happening to them?"

Ava flipped down the visor mirror and peered at her own eyes. To her surprise, she barely even recognized her reflection. Her eyes had become a vivid constellation of blues and yellows, and against her pale skin it created a ghostly, otherworldly look. The knot in the pit of her stomach that she had been trying to ignore all day doubled in size. It was impossible to avoid now.

With a sigh, Ava flipped the mirror back up and mumbled, "I wish I could say this was the weirdest thing that's happened to me today."

"You mean the thing with the ink in your hair?"

"No. Not even that. When I was swimming . . ." Ava started slowly. "I had these terrible pains in my hands and feet. And I saw things, like, really clearly—like, microscopic things in the water."

Kevin's brow furrowed in confusion. "Sounds like maybe you held your breath for too long and your brain got a little waterlogged?"

Kevin's words managed to pull a small smile from Ava. She blushed and muttered, "Shut up! I mean . . . I don't know, I can't explain it. It was just freaky."

"You've been under a lot of stress, Ava," Kevin said, taking her hand and rubbing the back of it with his thumb. "The way everyone was looking at you to win . . . I mean, people's brains can do wild things when they're stressed. Maybe you're a medical mystery, but chances are you're just an amazing swimmer who's really earned herself a break."

"Yeah, I guess that makes sense." Ava tried to tell herself that was all it was, but her words felt hollow. She wanted to believe Kevin's explanation, but she couldn't escape that little shard of doubt poking at the back of her mind.

"Honestly, I'm more worried about your eyes. I should probably take you home, it could be an infection or something."

"Yeah, that sounds good."

On the drive back, Ava couldn't help flipping the visor mirror down every few minutes to check her eyes in the mirror. The colors quickly faded and did not return. After a bit, he took her hand and held it. Having his hand on hers reminded Ava to breathe, and she turned her attention instead to the trees and the star-studded sky outside her window. Ava drifted off so deeply that she barely noticed when Kevin stopped the car.

"Ava," he said gently. She blinked and found herself back in the driveway of her home. It was hard to believe that she had been there just eight hours ago, feeling as though she knew exactly what the day would hold. As if he was reading her mind, Kevin leaned forward to kiss her tenderly on the forehead. "Go get yourself some rest, okay? I'll see you tomorrow."

"Thank you," Ava told him. She knew, somehow, that Kevin could understand everything she was trying to tell him with those two words. With a quick peck on his cheek, Ava slid out of the car and walked up to her home, casting one last look over her shoulder to see Kevin waving goodbye before driving off into the night.

Outside her house, Ava paused for a minute to catch her breath. If she told her mother all the strange things that had happened today, that would make it real. She would have to face the fact that something was happening, something might be wrong with her. Hoping to at least postpone the inevitable, Ava opened the door as quietly as she could and hurried up to her room. She only made it halfway up the stairs when a warm but commanding voice rang out from behind her.

"Don't even think about trying to avoid me."

Ava froze. Slowly, she turned around and found her mother, Sura, standing at the foot of the staircase. Sura had an athletic frame, striking silver hair, and emerald eyes that were currently giving her daughter a thorough scan. "You swam wonderfully! I'm so proud. But why do you look like the world is ending?"

"Um . . ." Ava paused. She didn't know how to answer that yet; she needed time to gather her thoughts. "Can I have a sec to change?"

"Sure, take your time." As Ava turned and started to make a break for her room, Sura's parting words echoed after her. "I'm not going anywhere!"

Ava rushed to her room before her mom could pry any further. After quickly swapping her damp clothes for some pajamas, she slipped into the bathroom to examine her eyes once more. As far as she could tell they were back to normal, with no traces of blue or yellow left amid the brown. Since Kevin had seen the change, too, she couldn't tell herself it had just been her eyes playing tricks on her, like what had happened in the pool. Satisfied, she walked back downstairs and hardly made it off the last step before her mom swept her into an enormous hug.

"With everything going on in our lives, I don't often remember to tell you how proud of you I am," Sura murmured, her cheek pressed against Ava's hair. She pulled back to look at her daughter and Ava caught a glimpse of tears glistening in her green eyes. "Watching you grow up . . . it's just breathtaking sometimes."

"Thanks, Mom," Ava mumbled. She had to avoid her mom's gaze so she wouldn't start crying herself. Honestly, seeing Sura cry was pretty out of character. "Are you okay?"

Sura shook her head and squeezed Ava's shoulder. "Yes, honey, of course. Come on, I ordered sushi. I figured you'd be hungry after such a long day."

"That sounds amazing, thank you!" Ava's stomach rumbled as if to back her up. She hadn't even realized how hungry she was until that moment, but Sura had reminded her how little she had eaten, and sushi sounded incredible. She opened the fridge to find two delicious looking spicy tuna rolls waiting for her. She couldn't resist. Ava grabbed the rolls and stuffed them piece by piece into her mouth without even bothering to sit down. Sura watched her quietly and, without any comment, offered Ava some of her own food. In the blink of an eye, Ava had scarfed that down, too. She looked up to find her mom still watching her and, defensively, she asked, "What? I was hungry, like you said!"

"I can see that! I was just wondering . . ." Sura paused, seemingly searching for the right words. "Why did you stop in the middle of the race?"

"Oh, uh, I just swallowed some water!" Ava said brightly. She hoped that her quick, easy answer would make her mom just move on.

But Sura just kept looking at her.

"Hmm," she said finally. "Alright. Well, wait here. I have something for you."

While Sura rummaged around upstairs, Ava ate every last grain of rice that had been left behind. When Sura came back, a small box in hand, Ava was surprised to find her mother tearing up again. This just went to show exactly how weird this day was. Sura was a sentimental person, sure, but she was one of the toughest people Ava knew. She couldn't remember the last time she had seen her mom cry, let alone twice in one night.

"Mom, are you sure you're okay?"

"Oh, yes. I'm just happy. You've grown up so much these past few years, and you're turning into such an incredible young woman . . . Okay, okay, enough of that." She dried her eyes with her sleeve, blowing out a quick breath. "Here's your birthday gift."

Sura handed Ava a tiny blue metal box, with a small shield carved into the lid. Inside, Ava found the most fascinating necklace she had ever seen. It was a silver pendant made of interlocking pieces that created the illusion that it was transparent, with small sapphires studding the metal. As Ava looked more closely, she found that the color within the gems seemed to almost be moving in waves. The thin metal made it appear delicate, but when Ava touched it, she found that it was much stronger than she'd expected. She clasped it around her neck and, as she let it drop, the hairs on her arms bristled and a chill ran down her spine.

"Oh . . . wow."

"This was given to me a long time ago by someone very special. Now it's yours," Sura told her.

"It's beautiful," Ava whispered, staring down at the pendant.

"Wear it in good health!"

Ava threw her arms around her mother and squeezed her tight. It was a beautiful mother-daughter moment, but then Ava felt her stomach rumble. She tilted her chin back and peeked up at her mom with a small, guilty smile. "Hey, uh, Mom? Is there any more sushi?"

Sura laughed and gave Ava a loud kiss on the forehead. "No. But I love you, and I love where your head is at. Let's order some more! It's your birthday, we should go all out."

As she dialed the sushi restaurant, Sura walked into the living room and Ava trailed behind her. She could hear her mom on the phone, chatting up the hostess that she'd become good friends with after ordering from them so often. Turning back to see Ava behind her, Sura gave her daughter a wink and quickly confirmed her order. She tossed her phone down and refocused on Ava. "While we wait, tell me more about your day!"

Ava struggled to find the words to describe the odd day she'd had. "Well . . . it was long, that's for sure. Amazing, but long. And . . . kind of weird?"

"Weird how?" Sura asked the question as if, somehow, she already knew the answer.

Sura was intuitive, often knowing what her daughter needed without Ava having to express it. But Ava was sure her mother couldn't possibly understand *this*. Ava wanted to tell Sura everything that had happened today, but she didn't want her to think she was crazy or rush her to the hospital.

"Just a lot of emotions, I guess," Ava said finally.

Sura studied her for a long moment, and Ava was sure she was going to get called out for lying. Instead, Sura said, "Well, you did have a very stressful day, so that makes sense. But remember that it was also a really successful one! You should be proud of yourself. And with your birthday being today, too, these changes make it even more special."

Changes, Ava thought to herself. That word seemed particularly purposeful with the looks Sura had been giving her and made her do a double take. *Does she know what's been happening to me?*

"Oh, seaweed," Sura muttered suddenly. Seaweed was her own special term for when she was frustrated. Ava never understood it, since they lived in a land-locked state, far from any ocean, but every time she heard it, it made her smile. "I forgot to make you a cake!"

Ava was so relieved that they were talking about normal things again that she couldn't even care about a birthday cake. "Don't worry about it! Sushi is the perfect birthday meal; I don't need anything else."

Ava sat back in her chair, absentmindedly twirling her new necklace between her fingers, while Sura started to pull up a movie. It was a tradition to watch the movie *Julia and Julia* on their birthdays. Ava loved cooking, and Sura had always said how important recipes were in passing down family traditions. Her thoughts started to spin over whether she should tell her mom about the true weirdness of the day.

Suddenly the doorbell rang, snapping Ava out of her thoughts but sealing her decision at the same time. As if Sura had read her mind, she looked over at Ava and said, "I'm just going to grab that and then we can talk, okay?"

The second Sura reentered the room, Ava's eyes grew wide, and she reached for the sushi bag like it was going to leap into her arms. Sura passed it to her and took her seat beside Ava. "So? Anything you want to talk about?"

"Oh, nothing," Ava replied without taking her eyes off the food. She ripped the bag open like she was ripping wrapping paper off a present, revealing the three sushi rolls hidden underneath. "Wow, I must be really hungry from all the swimming!"

"I can't blame you; you were really cutting through the water. You know, your dad and I were pretty great swimmers, too. Maybe that's where you get it from!"

Ava looked up from her sushi. Quietly, she said, "You haven't talked about him in a long time."

"It's hard for me to talk about him," Sura admitted. "He was the most wonderful man. He was my best friend and on days like this I . . . I miss him very much."

For the third time that night, Sura started to cry. Ava rushed forward to wrap her mother in her arms, trying hard to hide the anxiety coursing through her. Her own eyes started to water, and she pleaded, "Mom, please don't cry!"

They held each other close as Sura took a deep, shuddering breath, and then wiped her eyes. When she looked at Ava again, she had a bright smile on her face despite her watery eyes. "I must have had an emotional day, too. I'm gonna go get some sleep, but we'll talk more tomorrow, okay?"

"Sure, Mom. Sleep well!"

As her mother walked upstairs, Ava turned off the forgotten TV and turned her attention back to her sushi. She shoved the remaining pieces into her mouth like it was the last food on earth, barely stopping to think. Even when the last bits had been swallowed, she was still starving. She hurried to the fridge to see what else she could find to eat. The first thing she spied was her mom's famous meatloaf, which she normally would grab immediately, but for some reason, the smell made her want to gag. She shoved aside one thing after another in search of something that would satisfy her seemingly insatiable craving, but nothing was quite right.

Then she sniffed and smelled something delicious. Her hands moved as if they had a mind of their own, shoving aside bottles and bowls to grab something from the very back of the fridge. It was a jar of gefilte fish.

Ava had never liked it before. She'd seen her mom and their friends eating it during Passover a couple months ago, but since then, the stuff was relegated to the back corner of the fridge. It had always looked pretty nasty to her, like a fish meatball, swimming in discolored juice.

Now, though, it seemed like the most appetizing food in the world.

Ava cracked the jar open, and the smell that wafted out was so intoxicating that Ava started to pluck the slimy things out and eat them one after another, like popcorn. She didn't even stop to chew, letting them slide down her throat, one after another. With each bite, more and more energy returned. When she finally paused to take a breath, she caught a glimpse of her reflection in the stainless steel of the refrigerator.

Ava didn't even recognize herself. Her hair had turned from brown to shades of blue and purple; her eyes were blue and yellow once again. She gaped at herself, unable to comprehend the image staring back.

What is happening to me?

3

Blackout

The next morning, Ava came downstairs to find the empty jar of gefilte fish sitting on the counter—a reminder of her crazy craving. As she moved to throw away the jar, she saw a note scrawled in her mother's elegant handwriting:

Good morning, Ava,
I had to leave town to meet a friend. I know this is sudden, but I should be back sometime late tonight. Use my card to order anything you want. Call me if you need me.
Love you,
Mom

She stared at the note, and then at the empty jar. Her mother must've seen it.

She must think I'm going insane, Ava thought, rushing upstairs to get ready for school.

Since Kevin had chess club, Ava took the bus to school, making a beeline for the quiet of the back seat. Her eyes and hair were back to their normal colors, but her skin looked pale and waxy. When she arrived, she went straight to Room 305 and took her seat before the bell rang. Ava couldn't help but blush at seeing the joy on her classmates' faces.

The class quieted down when Mr. Thornbrook entered the room. Built like a football player and one of the savviest teachers in the school, Mr. Thornbrook was an intimidating figure. Even though he was a science teacher, he almost always incorporated lessons about math or history into his classes and liked to give what he called "fun facts." Ava tried to keep track, but she could swear Mr. Thornbrook just made up the numbers as he went. Yesterday they may have learned fun fact number eighteen, but a week before it was fun fact number twenty-nine.

Mr. Thornbrook got to his desk, put on his reading glasses, cleared his throat, and shouted, "We did it!"

Everyone cheered.

He pointed to Ava. "You did it! I am so proud of you, Ava." Mr. Thornbrook cleared his throat and straightened his posture. Fun fact number thirty: Ava is definitely the fastest swimmer in the world!"

The entire class started to whoop and holler.

"Okay, okay, let's get to it. I know we only have a few days left of school, but I wanted to go over the last of the curriculum. Today, we will touch briefly on evolutionary biology and Darwin's findings on the finches of the Galapagos Islands. We have already spoken about how the finches developed certain traits to help them thrive in their different environments . . ."

Usually, Ava was excited for this class, but today she was lagging, her eyes struggling to stay open. Trying to keep her mind from wandering, she raised her hand.

"Yes, Ava?"

"Could land animals develop traits such as webbed hands or the ability to see really well underwater?"

"Maybe if they were in the Marvel universe!" one student called out.

Ava glanced at the boy who had spoken, faked a laugh, and then turned back to Mr. Thornbrook.

After a moment, he spoke. "Yes, it can happen."

Ava's breath caught in her throat.

"But known cases are extremely rare, and usually it is due to a glitch in the DNA acquired before birth," he continued. "What I am talking about are traits that are beneficial to the offspring and then passed down to later generations. Webbed feet and hands are of greater benefit to an aquatic animal than a land-based animal. That's why we have lost those traits. Even for amazing swimmers like you, Ava. You live on land, so you evolved traits that best suit survival in your environment.

"Fun fact number twelve: Some animals, such as the peppered moth, can go through rapid mutations to help them survive. During the Industrial Revolution, the peppered moth went from having wings that were mainly white with black spots to being almost completely black. It had to make these physical changes to blend into its new smog-filled environment. Camouflaging, or blending into your environment, is a way to survive and thrive. If predators cannot see you, then you will live. Moths that remained mostly white were easily spotted and eaten by birds, so rapid natural selection took place. Generally speaking, creatures do not evolve or change rapidly during adulthood, but rather over the course of a few, or many, generations."

As the lesson continued, Ava fell silent, thinking of what had happened to her. The sound of the bell startled Ava so much that she jumped out of her seat, knocking her books to the ground.

A few kids laughed at her. Normally, she would've found it funny, too, but this time, she couldn't even bring herself to smile.

There was only one more class until lunch, but Ava was starving. Normally Ava loved having gym class, but as she made her way to the gym through the busy halls, she didn't feel strong enough to do a single pushup.

She struggled to open one of the two large blue doors that led to the locker room. It seemed so much heavier than usual, like someone was pushing back on it from the other side. Ava changed into her gym clothes and got in line with the other students, her vision swimming.

What is wrong with me? she thought, slapping, and pinching herself to wake up. *Snap out of it, Ava!*

She licked her lips, finding them so dry and cracked, like sandpaper. They burned, too. She desperately needed lip balm, but she didn't even have any in her bag. Her lips had been just *fine*, yesterday. What had she done to them?

As she sat there, gnawing on her painful lips, the gym teacher, Ms. Florence, flung open the heavy doors. Though she was only five-foot-three, the woman was a badass. Even Mr. Thornbrook, who towered over her, was scared of her. No one messed with Ms. Florence.

"Okay, class, today we're gonna stretch, run laps, then finish up with a game of dodgeball!"

Half the class cheered; the other half groaned. As the class started to twist and stretch, Ava lagged two steps behind her classmates. Each simple stretch took more energy to accomplish than the last. As she rose to her feet, her head spun, but she quickly regained her composure.

Ava left her mat to get some water from the drinking fountain at the side of the gym. Her dry lips throbbed with every breath as she bent down to take a sip of water. Ava kept her lips pressed tightly around the stream so as not to miss a single drop.

"That's enough, Ava! Get back over here!" yelled Ms. Florence.

Ava did not move. Instead, she gulped even more water.

"*Ava*! Get your butt back over here *now*!" Ms. Florence screamed.

The tone of her voice jolted Ava back to reality. When she finally stopped drinking, she licked her lips again.

They were fine. Not even a little chapped. It was as if they'd never been cracked at all.

Weird, Ava thought, licking them again as she fell in line with the other kids.

"Okay, enough stretching. Let's get to running!" Ms. Florence ordered.

Most of the students milled about on their way to the track like a herd of sheep, but Ava loved running. She usually led the pack, and today was no exception.

She started at the head of the pack, yet, as that incredible thirst returned, even worse than before, she quickly fell back to the joggers, then fell behind with the last group of students. When even those kids passed her, Ava stopped running. Out of breath, she gasped for air, and beads of sweat dripped from her chin.

She licked her lips and found them cracked again. It was so bad, she could taste the metallic tang of blood.

How did that happen?

When Ava made it to the starting line, Ms. Florence called her over. "Ava, what's wrong?"

"I need water," Ava wheezed. "I'm not feeling so good."

"Okay, go ahead," Ms. Florence conceded.

Ava couldn't get to the water fountain fast enough, but when it came into sight, she groaned in frustration. She couldn't stand the thought of sipping water that trickled from it. She wanted to chug it down by the gallon.

Ava trudged through the double doors into the hallway. A brightly lit vending machine beckoned her from the opposite wall. She breathed a sigh of relief when she reached her destination, but her face fell as she realized that she had left her wallet in her bag.

"Ava! Do you need money?"

Ava turned around to see one of her good friends, walking past, a backpack slung over her shoulder. "Elli! You're my hero!"

She reached into her bag and produced a couple of one-dollar bills. "Here you go."

Grateful, Ava shoved the money in the machine, pressed a button, and a large bottle of water popped out. Ava grabbed the bottle and chugged the entire thing in one enormous gulp.

When she finished, Elli was staring at her with slight horror on her face.

"Wow, I've never seen anyone drink that fast! What does Ms. Florence have you guys doing in there?"

Feeling stronger, Ava opened the large blue doors with ease. The class was already in the middle of the dodgeball game, and Ava could see that the red team was losing badly to the blue team.

"Ava, why don't you join the red team." Ms. Florence's tone made this sound more like a command than a suggestion. "They could really use your help."

Ava ran to grab a ball that was rolling toward her. She threw it as hard as she could, hitting the feet of a student from the blue team.

Ava retreated, distancing herself from the barrage of incoming dodgeballs. She launched a ball, hitting another blue team member in the arm. When she caught a glimpse of a ball heading right for her, she leapt into the air, successfully dodging a second ball headed for her legs.

"Nice, Ava!" one of her teammates shouted from the sideline.

She was so focused on not getting hit that she didn't realize she was the only person left on her team. Ava stood alone, facing three blue team members who snickered like hyenas.

As the next volley headed toward Ava, she leaped, dodged, and spun out of the way to avoid the hit.

"How did she do that?" a girl named Serena shouted.

Just then, a ball slammed into Ava's left thigh.

"You're out!" Ms. Florence yelled, as Ava looked around, stunned.

The blue team rushed to congratulate the kid who'd caught her off-guard, while the red team moaned. Breathing hard, Ava walked off the court, just as the bell clanged to mark the end of the period.

Ava was starting to feel faint and parched again, so she was eager to get to the cafeteria. She changed out of her jersey and rushed to refill her water bottle on her way to the cafeteria. Once she was in line to get her food, the options were less than appealing: burgers and fries, pizza, or spaghetti. They all looked disgusting, but she had to eat something.

Ava found Kevin saving a seat for her, and as always, he had a big smile on his face. But this time, he seemed even happier than usual. She plopped her tray on the table and slumped down next to him.

"Hey, you okay? You still don't look so good."

"I don't know . . . I don't feel well at all." Ava chugged her water. This time, it did not help.

"Why don't you try eating some food? Maybe you're hungry."

She took a bite of her burger and had a few fries. The first few bites only made her feel worse. What was going on with her? Was she coming down with something? Fries used to be her favorite food.

Ava set aside her food and frowned as her stomach flip-flopped like a dying fish.

"Hey. Why are you so happy?" Ava asked, hoping to keep her mind off the churning in her gut and the chills snaking their way down her spine.

"Just reliving last night."

"Yeah, me, too—over and over." She forced a smile. "Last night at the lake was so nice, Kev. It was the best part of the entire day."

"It really was," Kevin remarked. "Though I worry you might have made the sunset jealous with your beauty."

"Oh, stop it! You're such a cornball! Who says stuff like that?" Ava laughed, nudging him.

"Hey, it got you to laugh, didn't it?"

"Yes, it did. How do you always know how to cheer me up?" Ava's smile dissipated as she felt the blood drain from her face once again.

"Ava, you really don't look so hot," Kevin observed, putting a hand on her forehead.

"I don't feel so hot," Ava replied, trying to focus on her food. She tried to eat her fries and took another bite of her burger, but she was hit almost instantly with a wave of nausea.

"I think I'm going to be sick," Ava yelped. She stood quickly and ran to the bathroom.

She opened a stall door and crouched over the toilet to vomit. After flushing the toilet, she shuffled to the sink to wash up. As Ava threw water on her face, she caught a glimpse of herself in the mirror. Her skin had acquired a sickly yellow tinge, her hair was thin and lifeless, and her eyes were hazy. She began to feel a bit better with each splash of water on her face.

What the heck is going on?

"You got this—let's just make it home and call Mom," Ava reassured her reflection.

Kevin was waiting outside the bathroom door when she walked out.

"Did you get sick? How are you feeling now?" Kevin asked.

"I need to go home."

"I'll take you to the nurse."

"No! No nurse, we just need to get to your car, okay?" Ava demanded. She didn't want any nurse or doctor telling her she was a freak.

Kevin just nodded. "I'll drive you home."

Ava barely made it from Kevin's car to her front door before her vision started to blur. She used all her strength to unlock her door and wobbled inside. She heard Kevin pull away, but before she could scream for help, black spots obscured her sight entirely and Ava plummeted to the floor.

She was in a world of darkness for what seemed like ages. As she lay helpless on the ground, thoughts of her mother started to trickle through. Why wasn't her mother home yet? Where was she? As if she had summoned her, Ava heard the jingle of her mother's keys opening the door.

"Ava!" her mother shouted. "Don't worry, minnow, Mama's here, I've got you." Sura's sweet voice penetrated the darkness from somewhere far in the distance.

Ava groggily opened her eyes. "Mom? What's going on?"

"Don't worry, everything will be fine . . . just try to rest."

Ava's ears perked up when she heard the bathtub water running, She somehow found the energy to drag herself to the tub and climb in. In the cool water, her tense muscles slowly relaxed. Sura made a makeshift pillow out of some towels and propped Ava up against the edge of the tub so she could rest comfortably.

After what felt like only a few minutes, Ava awoke to the sound of her mother humming. Her eyes were closed, and her body was floating in the water. Ava's breathing was faint, like that of someone in a deep sleep.

"Mom?" Ava whispered as she opened her eyes.

"We had a bit of a scare, huh?"

"A bit?" Ava muttered in a sarcastic tone.

"We have a lot to talk about, Ava. Just know everything is going to be fine, and everything you have been feeling is normal."

"Something is definitely wrong with me, Mom. What's happening?"

"Nothing."

"Mom, look at me." She raised her voice in frustration. "Obviously something isn't right."

As Ava's vision cleared, she saw her mother smiling.

"I know what is happening to you, and I will explain everything. But right now, we have to get you back on your feet," Sura said. "Let's get you out of the tub—you've been in there for five hours."

Five hours? That's almost a full day of school.

"Get dressed and meet me in the living room. Everything will be okay." Sura paused. "Don't worry. You look fantastic."

Ava tried to sit up. *What does she mean, I look fantastic?*

She wasn't sure she wanted to know, so Ava did everything she could not to look at herself in the tub. She felt different, more powerful, more herself.

Ava stood up in front of the mirror, her eyes focused on the drain of the sink. She needed to build up the courage to look into the mirror. She knew she would look different; she could sense it. Her clothes still dripping, she raised her head.

Ava gasped. Her hair was as thick as seaweed, with shades of blue and purple. Her eyes were blue and yellow, with an orange tint around her pupils. Her skin seemed tougher, yet as smooth as satin. Ava traced her skin with her pointer finger, going over the raised fluorescent orange, blue, and purple patterns that resembled the most unique and beautiful henna designs. But as beautiful as they were, they were on her face, and *that* was far from normal.

Oh, no. What AM I?

4

Acathodian Blood

Ava slowly walked downstairs, knees still weak and hands shaking. Her mother was fixing a pot of tea, as if nothing was the matter.

Ava's words tumbled out before her feet reached the final step.

"Mom, what's wrong with me?"

Sura grabbed an afghan from the back of a sofa and wrapped her daughter in it, hugging her tightly.

"Nothing's wrong with you, sweetheart," Sura said in a calm voice.

"Mom? Hello? Look at me!" She pointed to her skin, swirling with bright colors.

Her mother didn't bother to look. "That's what happens when you're in the water. It fades as your skin dries out. But sit. I'm sure that's the first of many questions you might have."

Plopping herself down on her favorite leather chair, Ava pushed a button that made the leg rest spring out. After a hard day, this chair was the one place she could always come to feel grounded. When her mother handed her the tea, she cozied into her spot and let the sweet smell of the tea wash over her.

Sura swirled a spoon in her mug, collecting her thoughts. "I guess there is no good way to start this conversation, other than to tell you that everything you're going through is normal for our kind."

Ava nearly choked on her tea. "Sorry, did you say our kind? What am I, a mermaid?!"

"Oh no, dear, mermaids are pompous creatures! Well, some can be sweet." Sura couldn't hide her amusement.

"Wait—mermaids are real?" Ava's face went white.

"Yes, of course," Sura said dismissively. "But we belong to a long line of aquatic beings called Acathodians. For thousands of years, Acathodians have traveled between sea and land. Over time, many of us developed the ability to breathe air. Sadly, after years of staying on land, many were unable to return to the sea."

Ava's stomach twisted, as if the life she knew was slipping away.

"I know this is a lot to process. I'm sure it all sounds crazy right now. I totally understand that. But let me at least try to tell you everything I know, and then we can talk through some of your thoughts."

Acathodians. It sounded like a made-up word. Ava briefly wondered if her mother was simply losing it. But if so, she was, too—after all, she'd seen herself changing. She sipped her tea and nodded, signaling Sura to continue.

"Because so many Acathodians either wanted to or had to remain on land, the powers that be directed a group of people to help our kind get established here."

"What do you mean by 'the powers that be'?" asked Ava.

"Your great-great-great grandmother was sent as a leader to help the formation of our new world on land. It was an incredibly exciting time! Our family had the privilege of serving as the Elite Master Guard to Enzo, the ruler of Hadal, and his future kin. Before he became the headmaster, he and all who followed him rose within the Egerian Revolution, which sparked the War of Egeria . . ."

"Wait, hold on. That's way too much information. I have no idea what you're talking about. We need to take this slow. First question: were your people—"

"*Our* people . . ." Sura corrected.

"Were our people the first to inhabit the land? Like, are humans actually our people?"

"Well, yes and no. Man did evolve from Acathodians, but humans now are completely different beings."

Ava squinted, trying to wrap her mind around this impossible information. She hadn't learned any of this in science class. Nevertheless, she did some mental calculations.

"Wait . . . were Acathodians alive when dinosaurs roamed the Earth?"

Sura paused. "We are not that old, but let's focus on what is happening in the present first."

"Okay . . ."

"As you're starting to see, we are not human. We can pass as human—well, before we turn—but there is much more to each of us than any human could imagine."

"But . . . the way my hair and eyes have changed . . . Why don't you look like me?"

"Every Acathodian develops a different set of traits and abilities. Mine allowed me to adapt more quickly to land than most of our people."

"Was Dad one of us, too?" Ava blurted.

"Your father was a great Acathodian warrior who fought bravely by the side of our leader, Maridius." Sura had a far-off look, as if she was traveling deep into her memory. "He fought until his last breath."

"What happened to him? I mean, what really happened?"

"During the last great battle, we almost lost everything. Your father died protecting Maridius. I knew then that it was time to flee to land for good."

"Wait, why was there a battle? And what would have happened if you didn't flee?" Ava asked, still struggling to believe her mother's words.

Sura closed her eyes and took a shaky breath.

"I was so scared. You and I were completely alone. I didn't know if we would survive the journey, but we had no choice or else we would have been executed. I knew that if we could get safely to land, there would be other Acathodians there to keep us both safe."

Ava shook her head slowly, trying to absorb this information. "Hold up a minute. Have I lived in the water before?"

"Not exactly . . . you were born on land but blessed by the sea. I was pregnant with you when I fled. I know it's a lot to take in. You started to transform to your Acathodian ways during your championship race. We had no way of predicting how your transformation would take place, but I'm afraid it has happened much more suddenly than we expected. The scariest part for Acothodians is that there is no indicator of when or if the transformation may occur while on land. We were lucky to catch yours. You will need to learn about who and what you are, and, for that, I think your best chance of survival is to rejoin our people."

"Or what? I could die?"

"Tonight, you had a very close call, minnow. If I hadn't gotten you into that bathtub in time, you might have died." Sura took Ava's hand. "I'm sorry to be so blunt right now. I love you very much, and don't want to make your life harder . . . but sometimes we need to do things that we don't want to do. Part of me has been dreading this moment for years, all I ever wanted to do was to protect you. I will continue to do everything I can to keep you safe as you embark on this new stage in your life. You will face many difficult choices, but also some life-changing adventures. The best thing we can do right now is live in the moment and prepare for what's to come."

"What is to come?" Ava asked, wondering what could possibly be worse than this—turning into a fish, or hallucinating that she was turning into a fish. Either way, here she was, looking into her mother's eyes, hearing these crazy words from a woman who'd only ever told her the truth.

They will call me fish girl. Will I grow fins? Will I be able to speak to fish? Ava's thoughts spiraled down a winding path. "Am I supposed to fight in some kind of fish war?"

Her mother frowned. "No . . . Ava. I am being completely honest. Look at you, this is not a joke."

Ava snorted as a wave of anger swept over her. Of course, it wasn't a joke. This was the furthest thing from funny.

"I can't even look at you right now. If this is true and I am an 'aco'-whatever, then why did you not prepare me for this? Like, where the heck do I go from here? Fish land? This is all so stupid and ridiculous! What's next? I also have lizard cousins?"

Her mother gave her a disappointed look. "I am sorry, Ava, a mother only does her best and there is a lot you cannot understand just yet. You are going to the Land School. We should move as soon as possible."

"Land School . . ." Ava robotically repeated out of pure shock, unable to fully comprehend this news. "What do you mean? I *am* going to a school on land."

"No. Land School is a special school where you will evolve and be taught the Acathodian ways. It's the safe space that your great-great grandparents helped establish for our kind. It is also where I fled to after the war."

Ava recoiled as if she'd been punched in the chest. "Why do I need to go?"

"You need to develop the ability to evolve. I had to do the same. I did not always look like this."

"So, you're saying that if I stay on land right now, I die? What about my friends? What about Kevin?"

"First things first—you are not going to die! We caught your transformation in time. You need to go to a special school for our kind, where you will grow to your full potential."

"I can't believe this is happening!" Ava crumpled over her lap, pressing her face into her hands.

"I know, it isn't fair. I know you're missing out on a lot. In an ideal world, I would like to see you finish up the last few days of your regular school year, but . . ." Sura hesitated.

"What if I don't go?" Ava asked.

"Well, there would be two possibilities. The first would be that your body won't handle the stress of such a profound genetic change. That can go in many directions, none of them good. The second is that you might be physically able to stay on land, but you would be targeted for looking so different and, most likely, dissected in the name of science."

"Oh great, so nothing too horrible, then," Ava mumbled, rolling her eyes. "Can I at least finish my last week of school? I need to say goodbye to everyone. Especially Kevin."

"You have three days of school left. We will assess how you are doing day by day. When I saw you swim, I had a feeling that your transformation was starting, so I immediately scheduled a meeting with the headmaster and secured your spot at the Land School. The headmaster knows you will be arriving within the week."

Sura drew Ava into a hug. "I know how crazy this all sounds. And I'm sorry I couldn't have prepared you better for it. It may seem like you're the only person in the world going through this, but I had the same feelings when it happened to me. And, while it's not clear to you right now, you are in for a spectacular adventure."

"The adventure I was expecting was senior year, a promposal, a limo ride . . . " Ava muttered, thinking of all the nights she'd dreamed about putting on a gorgeous dress and wowing Kevin's socks off. She might as well kiss going to prom with Kevin goodbye. "It's not going to happen, is it?"

"I know you wanted it, but honey, it's not something we can control. I promise everything will be okay."

Ava's mother kissed the top of her head and left her alone to process her new life.

Ava sat on her bed, staring into space as she replayed her conversation with her mother in her mind. Everything she thought she knew had been wrong.

But now, as she thought about it, it almost made sense. She wondered why she hadn't questioned it before. She'd always been attracted to the water. Her mom used to have to drag her from the ocean when she was a child.

Ava looked in the mirror and took in her new look. She combed through her hair with her fingers. It was the same thick hair that she knew, but the bright blue and purple were definitely striking. Different, but beautiful, too, in a way.

But "different" didn't even begin to cover the fluorescent henna-looking combination of orange and blue designs that now tattooed her skin. It was everywhere, from head to toe, even on her belly. She felt like she was permanently stuck in a skin-tight Halloween costume.

Reluctantly, Ava got two big duffel bags out of her closet to begin packing up her life for Land School. As she brought them to the center of her room, she tripped over one of the bags and fell to the floor. She lay there, unwilling to get up, and looked at the ceiling. Focusing on her wooden ceiling fan, Ava's head continued to spin along with it.

My whole world is turning upside down.

When she finally resolved to get up, she admired the photos on the wall over her bed. Each picture brought back happy memories. Taking each one in, she felt her eyes tearing up.

Blinking away the tears, she caught sight of a scribble she'd made on the wall as a kid. It was a rudimentary child's crayon drawing, and yet, now, as she looked at it more closely, she realized the lines resembled something.

They looked uncannily like the intricate patterns glowing from her skin.

She stared in awe, remembering when her mother had found it. She hadn't been upset. In fact, she'd loved it so much that she insisted it stay.

All this time, her mother had known. And yet she'd kept it to herself. Now, she was about to have the worst summer of her life. And it was all because of this family secret.

Clenching her hands into fists, she stomped over to her mother's room. Ava took a deep breath and barged in. "Mom, I—"

She stopped when she realized her mother was sitting on the edge of her bed, crying.

"Are you okay?" Ava rushed to her mother.

"Yes, love, just processing all these emotions." Her mother hugged her once again.

"Mom, will I ever see my room again?"

Ava's mother started to cry even harder. "Oh, minnow. I hope you will, some day."

She looked down at herself. "How am I supposed to go to school tomorrow looking like this? I can't look like this during my evolutionary biology class; my teacher will try to dissect me!"

They both let out a laugh.

"Don't worry, we will keep you away from water long enough to say goodbye to your friends," her mother whispered in her ear. "I will warn you, it is not going to be comfortable, so we need to make this a timely departure."

She nodded, trying harder to accept it, now that she knew it wasn't easy for her mother, either. "This is so stressful. I am trying not to freak out. So, I guess I should get used to this as the new me."

"As weird as it looks to you now, this is our normal." Sura smiled. "Okay, let's both get some sleep. It's been an intense evening."

Ava walked back to her room and turned off the lights. She had plastic glow-in-the-dark stars on her ceiling from when she was a child, and she was amazed that they still had the strength to glow after all these years. She found comfort in her stars. With each breath her eyelids got heavier, until she fell into a deep sleep.

5

Parting White Lies

The first thing Ava did when she woke was scramble to the mirror. She let out a sigh of relief. Her hair and eyes were back to brown. Her skin had turned a pale white, just a bit more flushed than her normal fair skin complexion. She'd be able to pass as normal. At least for now.

As Ava slowly moved about, her mind seemed detached from her body. She felt like a walking zombie, with the goal of just making it through today. However bad yesterday had been, she knew that today would only be worse. Today she had to say goodbye to Kevin. She couldn't tell him the whole truth—in fact, she wondered if what Sura told her even was the truth. But how could she lie to him? Ava journeyed downstairs, her legs moving faster than she wanted them too.

"Be brave!" Sura's voice assured her.

"As if I have a choice?" Ava shot back.

"You do have a choice, Ava. I just hope you make the right one."

"Not much of a choice, Mom. Stay and die or maybe be dissected in a lab or go to a freakshow of a school and live."

Her mother pinched her lips.

"You know what, whatever, I got to go," Ava quickly stated, grabbing her backpack, and heading for the door before her mother could respond.

"I hope I don't turn into a fish on the way there," Ava mumbled.

"You won't turn, Ava. But you might get very ill. If you do, call the nurse, and I'll come get you. Do what you need to do, and I will see you soon."

Walking through the front doors of Noblesville High, she was keenly aware of her laughing peers and the echoes of lockers opening and shutting in the halls. Ava had never really noticed the sounds until today, but she felt grateful for the sense of normalcy. The banner reading "Go, Piranhas Go!" still hung over the trophy case. Bright lights made the school feel alive. Ava stood next to her locker, absorbing this moment.

Suddenly a pair of hands covered Ava's eyes.

"Guess who?" a playful voice spoke into Ava's ears.

"Ummm . . . Russell?"

"No! Ha . . . What?"

"Relax, Kev. I knew it was you, who else would it be?" Ava teased, but the moment she turned around to look at him, she felt a stab in her heart.

"I knew that! Are you feeling better?" Kevin asked, putting an arm around her.

She stiffened. "Kevin, we need to talk."

The color drained from Kevin's face. "Uh-oh."

The stab in her chest only worsened. But it wasn't that bad. People did long distance relationships all the time. It wasn't the end. Or . . . was it? She had convinced herself that moving away didn't mean breaking up, but denial could only work for so long.

"What? No, I just wanted to tell you . . . you have a little dirt on your face." She wiped his cheek. "Right here."

Maybe living in a world of denial was the best plan after all. At least for a little while longer.

"Thanks, Ava," Kevin hesitantly replied, wiping at his cheek.

The bell above them clanged. Ava gave Kevin a quick peck on the cheek and raced off to math class.

As she slid into the room, she couldn't believe this might be the last time she would walk these halls or sit at her desk.

"So, you know the drill, last week of school, relax, and watch the movie," Mr. Wiseman began.

Ava quickly lost her focus on the film, wondering instead how she was going to break the bad news to Kevin.

I'll just tell him that my mother got a new job far away and we're moving, and we need to end things because I don't know when I'll see him again.

The bitter words cycled through her mind. It wasn't a solution; it was a lie.

And it was ending things, which was the last thing she wanted to do.

It would destroy Kevin, almost as much as it would destroy her.

Ava's heart squeezed in her chest as she walked down the hallway. She paused in front of the trophy case. She gazed at all the ribbons, medals, and trophies. Standing front and center was the trophy her team had just won.

But what Ava thought of was not the victory, but the memories—memories of laughter, adventures, and, of course, love. Emotions warred inside her as she continued down the hallway and into her very 'normal' classroom.

Ava sat in the same chair that she had sat in for the entire year. She remembered how squeaky and uncomfortable it was when she first started the year, but now, the chair was as cozy as a warm glove on a snowy cold day. Would she ever get used to Land School? Would it be like her current school, except filled with Acathodians? Would the school look different? Smell different? Would she be able to make friends there?

"Hi, Ava! I'm truly sad that today is your last day."

She looked up to see Mr. Thornbrook smiling at her. The words caught her off guard. How could he know? She had just found out herself. How could one of her teachers be in on the secret so soon?

"Oh! I didn't know you knew. But yeah . . . it's definitely a bummer."

"Well, don't worry. I'm sure a new adventure awaits."

"Well, Mr. Thornbrook, I just wanted to thank you for a wonderful year. I learned a lot." she said sincerely.

"Thank you, Ava, that's very kind of you to say. Don't worry, you will be in good hands," Thornbrook assured with a wink.

Why does he seem to know something I don't?

"Kevin!" Ava yelled down the hall.

Kevin threw his books into his locker and met Ava midway in the crowded hallway.

"Kevin, I really do need to tell you something important," she said breathlessly.

"Yeah, I figured," he sighed. "Is everything okay, Ava?"

Ava bit her lip, trying to think of the best way to break the news.

"You're freaking me out a bit here." Kevin's voice held a more serious tone.

"Sorry."

"What's really going on, Ava?" Kevin looked even more concerned this time.

"I have to move . . ." was all she could say.

His eyes went wide. "What? Okay . . . where to?"

"I got into this new school . . . it's important to my mother. It's eight hours away." The words tumbled out incoherently, the big lie she'd crafted falling apart as she said the words.

Kevin frowned. "A new school? And you want to go to it?"

"I don't have a choice," she said honestly.

He leaned against his locker and seemed to shrink. "Okay. What does that mean for us?"

"Kevin, you know I love you . . . I hope you do . . . but I don't know. I honestly don't. I mean, this might be the last time we see each other." Ava started to tear up.

Kevin took a sharp breath. "Okay, let's not get carried away. People do long-distance relationships all the time. Remember my cousin? He did long distance for a whole year! What we have is special, Ava . . ."

"I know, but this is different . . ."

He snorted. "No, listen to me. How is it different, Ava? It's eight hours away, not on a different planet!" His eyes narrowed. "Sure, it's hard, but I'm willing to make it work. The only way it wouldn't is if *you* didn't want to."

"Kevin, it has nothing to do with what I want or what you want. I really thought we could be together forever . . ."

". . . as long as we're in the same place? How is that fair? You don't even want to try?" Kevin shot back, his face reddening. "You're saying you want to break up. Is that it?"

She couldn't bring herself to say the word. Instead, she looked away. "Kev, I know this is hard, and you have every right to be angry, but—"

"But, what? What, Ava? You wake up one day and make this decision like I was never important to you." Kevin's voice cracked.

"Don't say that. You're the most important person to me," Ava admitted.

She had no idea what else to say. She had known this would be hard, but she hadn't been prepared for the extent of his anger.

"Okay . . . there's more. I haven't said anything because . . ." She paused. She hadn't wanted to lie to him, and so far, she hadn't. But she couldn't take the way she was looking at him. She had to find a way to smooth things over. "Kevin, I'm sick. I need to go to a specialized school for help. I can't say more than that right now, but please try to understand. I am so sorry. This isn't easy for me, either."

His mouth fell open. For a moment, he was clearly at a loss for words. She couldn't blame him. Sick people didn't win swimming championships. "What do you mean, you're sick?"

"You saw the changes in me. My eyes, my hair, how lethargic I was?"

"Your skin was very pale, and kind of . . . waxy looking. That's why I was so worried . . . You went to the doctor? What did they say?"

She nodded. "They said they don't know what it is, Kevin. But that I need help."

"Well, then I'll visit you there! It's not contagious, is it?" he asked, trying to hold her.

She squirmed away from his grip. "No, but . . . this isn't just a simple move."

"I don't care, Ava, I want to see you. I will always want to see you."

This back and forth could go on forever. It was clear that they loved each other. Of course, he was going to put up a fight. It was now or never . . . her moment to be blunt.

She held up her hand and gritted her teeth.

"Kevin, I am sorry. I don't know how else to say this, but we need to break up. Something huge and weird is happening to me. It's time for us both to get on with our lives."

The expression on his face—pure disappointment— made her want to take those words back. She only half-believed them, anyway. At that moment, she didn't know anything. If he'd tried to convince her to stay, she probably would've caved.

But he didn't. He simply shrugged and turned on her. "Whatever Ava . . . it seems like you've made up your mind."

There was so much more to say, but she couldn't. As Kevin walked away, Ava knew this moment would be her last memory of him. And it was a terrible one. She fought the tears that waited just behind her eyelids.

She didn't see any point in finishing the day. She had done what she needed to do. This horrible, hollow feeling would be her only reality as long as she stayed in those halls. Ava started to walk toward the exit, wishing she'd never come back here in the first place.

"Excuse me! Where might you be going, young lady?" the school guard inquired.

"I'm fine. I just need to go." She picked up the pace.

"Are you okay? Are you sick?" the guard questioned.

Ava did not respond. Instead, she walked right by the guard and opened the doors leading to the parking lot.

She had a new life to begin, whether she wanted to or not.

6

A Long Trip

Ava was numb and sick of crying by the time they got on the road. They left Noblesville and passed through the next town, Zionsville. Ava knew this town well. Her swim team regularly competed against their high school. As quickly as memories leapt into Ava's head, her future was racing ahead even faster. A feeling of powerlessness came over Ava—the inability to control time. She desperately wanted to stop time, even catch it in her hand, but the car kept racing forward.

Her mother wasn't helping. Sitting in the driver's seat, she focused straight ahead, driving over the speed limit and constantly looking in the rear-view mirror, as if someone was chasing them.

"Mom," she said, hugging herself. "You're not making this any easier."

"Ava, look in the mirror," her mother said, carefully choosing her words.

Ava flipped down the visor mirror. Her eyes were again hazy and white, her skin growing waxy.

"First, you'll begin to lose all your color, and then you'll go blind. You will be in terrible pain and start to break down from the inside out." Sura gave her a minute to take this in. "Yesterday, when I said you had some time, I was being too optimistic. This is an urgent situation, I'm afraid. You need to be with people who are like you—like us. It's the only way you can be safe."

"Well if I need to be with my people, why did you bring me to Indiana in the first place? Did you bring me here just so you could eventually yank me away from my life and my home?"

"The truth is a part of me didn't want you to change. Part of me hoped you wouldn't." Her voice was filled with sadness.

Ava snapped the sun visor back up. As beautiful as she thought the Acathodian appearance was, with their brightly hued skin and majestic eyes, she didn't feel that way. She felt freakish, as if she was transitioning into a corpse. But maybe, if she did as her mother said, she would be one of them . . .

Somewhere, an inkling of new pride was trying to push through. Ava caught her mother's remorseful expression, but that was the last thing she wanted to think about.

"The anger will subside . . . sadness will come again . . . happiness and love will flourish . . . and adventure will take hold," Ava's mother said.

"What was that—some sort of inspirational quote? Did you get that from a fortune cookie?" Ava blurted.

"I assure you that you will understand its full meaning soon enough," Sura said.

Ava stared out of the window and silence filled the car. The exhaustion of the last few days overcame her. Even though she didn't feel like relaxing, she knew that a rest would do her good.

"Go to sleep, love, everything will be fine."

Ava's mother started to hum a sweet lullaby, one that she'd always sung, ever since Ava was a small child. It made Ava feel slightly more at ease. But only slightly.

Ava jolted awake in her seat.

"Did you have a bad dream, minnow?"

"I just had a horrible nightmare," Ava quavered, choking for breath.

"What was it?" Sura glanced over at Ava.

"I was at school and, at first, it was so relaxing. There was a beautiful bird flying in the air outside the window . . . but then everything got weird and dark. There were horrible voices saying terrible things to me, and then I saw a figure . . ."

"And?"

"The figure was . . . me."

Ava looked out the window again. She didn't recognize where they were. The trees seemed taller, with leaves of many beautiful shades. The road in front of them was sleek and black, very different from the gray roads that defined the highways near home.

"Are we getting close?" Ava asked.

"We still have two more hours of driving."

Ava's body tightened with anxiety. The locked doors of the car felt like bolts on a prison cell, and her mother was the guard.

"I know . . . but it will be well worth it."

"What's it like at the Land School?" Ava asked. Whether because of the change of scenery, the distance, or her nap, curiosity once again started to creep back into her thoughts.

"It's magical, every inch is magical," Sura stated with a nostalgic smile.

Ava sat up a little taller.

"So why not just live there?" Ava questioned.

"It's not a city, Ava, it's a school, and both of us were human at the time, so there was no need to live there. As I told you, I was raised on land for the first several years of my life. When I was a little girl, we made the same trip to the Land School for help—just like you are now. I learned many things there about the Acathodian way of life. Then, when I was twelve, I went to my new home in Hadal. That's when I met your father." Sura took a second to look into Ava's eyes. "After you complete your training, you will move to Hadal as well."

"Wait, pause, stop. What is Hadal?"

"You are not sick, you're changing," Sura said.

"Stop the car," Ava demanded.

Sura kept driving, ignoring Ava's words.

"Stop the car and let me out."

"I am not doing that, Ava."

"You never said anything about Hadal. What is that?"

Sura paused, then spoke with surprising passion. "Hadal is an extraordinary, otherworldly, and mystical underwater city. It's an amazing place. And . . . it's not far from where we are heading now."

Ava sat back in her seat, unable to speak. The words were chained to her throat. She took a deep breath. "What else should I know?"

"A lot," Sura stated bluntly. "You'll learn so much at school. But in short, we have a long and complex history. Our people are tens of thousands of years older than humans. When Acathodians began to settle on land, they set up communities, some near the water and others far inland. As centuries passed and many new generations were born, these early Acathodians saw the evolution of humankind."

"This is totally crazy!" Ava said, not sure she wanted to believe it.

"Yes, it definitely is!" Sura's laugh acknowledged this truth, before she continued with a more serious tone. "I'm hardly an expert on our history, but there is one thing you should know, as time went on, the Acathodians on land became the humans you know today. Most of us forgot all about our Acathodian ways. Humans started to destroy the land, and their wreckage started to seep into our part of the world. This abuse of the land and sea caused a divide within our people. Our leader at the time, Isabella, wanted to destroy the human race and repopulate the land with new Acathodians."

Ava's eyes widened. "That's awful! How did she get away with this?"

"She didn't. The first rebellion occurred in an underwater city, Egeria. This sparked the first Acathodian war. The rebels successfully dethroned Isabella, and we elected Enzo as our new ruler."

"Did you fight in this war?" Ava asked.

"Oh no, Ava, this war took place thousands of years ago."

"That's intense!" Ava gasped. Maybe it was information overload or just exhaustion from everything that took place the last couple of days, but Ava no longer felt like talking, or thinking. Her mind journeyed to the sight of exquisitely beautiful trees with amber bark that whizzed by. The tall trees were covered with leaves which held more color than Ava had ever seen before. The leaves were vibrant shades of red and yellow along with vivid greens. If she squinted as they drove past, it looked as if the trees were on fire. At the base of the trees was the whitest earth she had ever seen.

"Mom, what's with the white dirt?"

"That's actually a unique kind of sand," Sura answered.

"I've never seen anything like it before. It looks so . . . fine. Like powder."

Her anger had miraculously been replaced with wonder. She sensed that they must be getting closer to their destination.

"How are you feeling over there? Is that a smile I see on your face?"

"I don't know . . . I feel excited and strangely powerful. I felt like this when I was swimming in my last competition. I didn't recognize it until just now. It's . . . amazing."

"I know just what you mean," Sura nodded. "Every time I make this drive, I feel the same way. It's proof of the power of our people—the closer we get to our own, the stronger that feeling becomes."

As Ava rolled down her window, she could smell the sea, the sand, the trees, and . . . something else she never smelled before. It was sweet and reminded Ava that she was hungry. She caught her reflection in the side view mirror. Her skin was changing into the fluorescent orange and blue she had seen after her night in the bathtub.

She was glowing! She watched in real time as her eyes went from brown and white to light blue and yellow with an orange ring around the pupil. Her hair grew thicker, painted with dark purple and blue streaks. The more she saw herself this way, the more beautiful she felt.

She wasn't sick. She was being healed.

The car made one final turn and then the road in front of them unfolded straight as an arrow, with an arcade of those flaming trees on each side. Ava could just make out something big in the distance. The car approached an imposing black gate adorned with a familiar emblem. She gripped her pendant.

"Mom, that's the same symbol that's engraved on the necklace box you gave me."

"It is the mark of our people—the Symbol of the Shield." Sura wore a big grin. "Wear it proudly, and never take it off. It gives you strength."

Ava rolled down her window and closed her eyes. She took a deep breath and exhaled.

A powerful gust of cool air rushed into the car, blowing Ava's and Sura's hair. The breeze grew in intensity, rattling the car with shocking force. Fear started to creep into Ava's soul. She tried desperately to call for her mother, but the wind took her voice, and the words never made it past her lips. As Ava's hair flung through the air and into her face, she caught a glimpse of her mother laughing as if she was riding a rollercoaster. What seemed so scary to Ava, was magical to her mother. And just like that, all of Ava's fears vanished while watching her mother's joy. The wind soon subsided to a cool calm breeze, and the sound of Ava's breath filled the void.

It was then, when silence filled the air, that the gate slowly swung open.

7

The Land School

Sura drove slowly. As they entered the property, the scenery shifted. The trees outside the gate had been vividly colored, but Ava now found herself surrounded by something darker. It was still incredibly beautiful, but in a more elegant and mysterious way. Intoxicatingly beautiful and majestic black trees sprang up along the road, their leaves streaked with amber, green and white. Some of the wood even glimmered, as if crystallized.

"Mom, what is that?" Ava leaned out of the window to gawk at the jewel-like trunks. "Those trees look like they've died and come back to life!"

"That's petrified wood," Sura replied. "Isn't it beautiful?"

"I've never seen anything like this." Awestruck, Ava felt her excitement building in her chest.

"Ava, there's an entire world you haven't seen yet. Just wait until we get inside!"

"I can't believe this is real," Ava whispered.

She was so captivated by the scenery that she almost failed to notice The Land School looming in the distance. As the car drew closer, the sounds of teenagers laughing filled the air. Ava shot a quick smile to her mother. For the first time in a while, she felt like everything was going to be just fine.

When, at last, they pulled up to the front entrance of the school, Ava's jaw dropped. The outer walls were made of petrified wood and old gray stone. The wood had the same glorious veins of crystal that Ava had seen lining the driveway, and the fine stone looked as though it would be more suitable for a castle than a school.

"Sura!" a tall, thin man called out from the front door. Grinning from ear to ear, he rushed to the car to give Ava's mother a hug.

"Ezra, it is so good to see you!" Sura said, returning the smile.

Ezra's skin was blue with yellow stripes, his eyes large and green. His dark, thick lips contrasted with his hair, which had been styled into several tiny silver spikes. Ezra walked toward Ava with his hand extended to introduce himself. With eyes wide, she shook his hand, realizing that the texture of his skin felt just like her own.

"Hi, Ava. It's so nice to finally make your acquaintance," Ezra said in a deep, calming voice.

"Hello . . ." She wanted to say more, but her vocal cords froze.

"You didn't think you were the only Acathodian in the world, did you?" Ezra responded to Ava's gawking.

"To be fair, I didn't think I was anything but human," Ava quickly responded.

"Indeed." Ezra turned to Sura. "I can't believe how much she looks like Ryker."

"You knew my father?" Ava blurted out.

"He was one of my closest friends."

"I remember the two of you fishing and seeing who could snag the biggest catch," Sura said with a laugh.

"Ah, the good old days. I miss him all the time." Ezra's voice softened. His face lit up with excitement as an old memory resurfaced. "Oh, man! Ava, there was one time your father and I almost got eaten by a great white shark and had to swim for our lives!"

"How did you get away?" Ava asked.

"Ha! Yeah, Ezra, how did you escape?" Sura chided, innocently elbowing him in the ribs.

"Your mother came to our rescue . . ." he said, somewhat sheepishly.

"You got that right!" Sura said with a hint of pride in her eyes.

"Your badass mom tackled the shark with such force that she nearly sent it flying out of the water."

She gave him a look. "No need to exaggerate, Ezra."

"Well, I will say this: I've never seen a great white shark swim away from an Acathodian that quickly."

"Mom, you tackled a great white shark?" Ava asked, eyes wide.

Sura shrugged. "Sometimes you do crazy things to protect the people you love."

"Will I ever be able to do something like that?" Ava asked, her mind wandering back to Kevin. She already missed him so much and wanted to tell him everything. But they'd left on such bad terms. *What is he doing now?*

Ezra presented the place to her like a valuable prize she'd just won. "How would you like a tour of the school, Ava?"

Ava's focus returned to Ezra's striped face, and she put on a smile. "Sounds great. Where to first?"

Once through the main door, they found themselves walking down a long hallway past arched wooden doors lining each side. Light shone down from a series of glass chandeliers that looked like smaller versions of the grand one in the lobby. When Ava looked down at the floor, she came to a sudden halt. A mosaic of complex, webbed patterns created an illusion that made her feel as though she were walking over empty space. The masterfully crafted marble flooring must have taken years to complete. Surrounded by gray brick walls, Ava couldn't help but feel that she had gone back in time to the age of European castles.

Ezra stopped at one of the arched doors, this one made from completely white wood. The wood didn't appear to be painted or stained, but somehow glowed. Ava had never seen anything like it.

"I know leaving your friends and old life behind is hard, but I promise you will begin to feel at home here soon."

Ezra opened the door to reveal the most breathtaking saltwater pool.

"Your mother told me you like to swim." Ezra's face made a knowing smirk.

Ava almost cried at the sight of it. The humongous natatorium made the Olympic pool from her championship look like a kiddie pool. On the far side of the room, an entire wall of floor-to-ceiling windows showed a body of water that extended as far as the eye could see. Where the water met the sky, Ava saw birds flying freely among puffy white clouds. The other walls were built from multicolored stone, reflecting sunbeams that bounced off the water. A blue light illuminated the smooth amethyst geode floors, causing them to sparkle. The remarkable sight reminded Ava of one of her favorite paintings: Starry Night. For a moment, Ava's worries evaporated. This room was the most beautiful thing she had ever laid eyes on. This was her Sistine Chapel, her Grand Temple, the place sculpted just for her.

"Do you like it?" Ezra asked.

"It's amazing! I've never seen anything so beautiful in my whole life."

He smiled. "It's great to rediscover this room through a fresh pair of eyes. You can come here almost any time you want."

"Well, if you ever don't know where to find me, I'll definitely be here."

"You would be surprised by how empty it can get. Some nights you could have this place all to yourself."

Sura's stomach rumbled, breaking the spell. "Oh, seaweed," she said, clamping a hand over her growling belly with a laugh. "Not to drag you from this lovely place, but is anyone else hungry?"

Ava nodded eagerly. "Definitely!"

She had been dying to discover the source of the delightfully sweet scent that had been wafting through the air ever since they had entered the building. The trio left the pool room and made their way to the dining hall. The rest of the hallway featured stained glass windows with abstract designs. The vibrant yellows, blues, and reds seemed to amplify the sweet smell as they entered the dining hall.

Five enormously long tables made of petrified wood were filled with chattering students. At the far end of the hall, an even larger table sported heaping plates of food, ready for the taking. A chef stood nearby with a large knife and fork, serving each student whatever dish they fancied.

Opposite the buffet was a smaller table which should have seated five or six people. No one was sitting there, but it was obvious to Ava that this table was for Ezra and his staff. Raised on a platform overlooking the student tables, the staff table had two tall candlesticks at each end. Three portraits hung from the wall behind it. A picture of an older-looking, mustachioed man with gray skin occupied the middle. The photo to the right was of Ezra. On the left, a woman stood tall, regally holding a staff. Her skin was green and yellow with hints of blue. As she walked closer to the table, she noticed that the Acathodians in the portraits all had big, beautiful eyes of multiple colors.

Ava's attention shifted to the students milling around the tables and eating their meals. This was the first time she had seen other Acathodians her own age. Some students looked almost human while others, perhaps more fully evolved, didn't resemble humans at all. Some students' skin had an iridescent sheen, which shifted rapidly between colors as the light hit them from different angles. Others had shark-like skin, while yet others were green and slick like eels.

As she continued to observe the scene, Ava noticed two students with webbed hands. Their hair was thick and curled like seaweed and their skin was as vibrant as her own. Whether tall or short, muscular or puffy, scaly or spiky, Ava knew that the students had one thing in common. They were Acathodian, just like her.

Ava followed her mother and Ezra to the food table. When they reached the buffet, she realized what the intoxicating smell had been. There was salmon, tuna, eel, shrimp, lobster, and three different kinds of soup.

"Smells amazing, doesn't it?" Ezra said, passing her a plate.

"It sure does!"

Her mouth watering, Ava took no time in piling the deliciousness onto her plate. For a moment, she thought back to Kevin, and how he hated seafood. To think, she'd once thought he was her perfect match. But the more she saw this place, her place, the more she realized how different they were.

"Hey! Ava!" Sura called.

She and Ezra had taken a seat at one of the long tables, and Ava walked over to join them. She started to pick at her food slowly, but soon couldn't help herself. Ava began shoveling forkful after forkful of fish into her mouth as if she hadn't eaten in days. Out of the corner of her eye, she noticed Ezra passing her mother an envelope made of metallic blue paper that almost looked like glass.

"It's from Maridius," Ezra said quietly.

Sura glanced up at Ezra before opening the letter. Ava watched her mother take a deep breath. As she read the letter, a few tears escaped down her cheeks.

Ava stopped her fish-laden fork in midair and quietly placed it back on her plate. "Mom . . . Are you okay?" Ava mumbled with a mouthful of food.

"Yeah, I'm fine, sweetie." Sura swiped a finger under her eyes. "I'm just happy to hear from an old friend."

She turned to Ezra. "Please tell him I will and thank you."

He nodded, and Ava returned to stuffing her face with slices of white-fin tuna.

Ezra chuckled. "So, I'm guessing you like the food?"

Ava realized he was watching her gulp down food like a seal at an aquarium and blushed, hot and hard.

"It's alright, Ava, you're not the first newcomer to eat ravenously in front of me. You're actually slower than most," Ezra laughed. "No need for manners here. Scarf away!"

"Ahm tffrying!" Ava said through a mouth full of tuna wrapped in seaweed. Once she had swallowed her food, she straightened her posture. "It is very nice to be here—strange and surreal, but nice. And I'm not just saying that because of the food."

"We're honored to have you," Ezra said. "Your family has always been very important to me. They're important to everyone, really."

"Except humans. Humans don't know about this place, right? How have you managed that? It's so incredible!"

"We are more hidden than you think. Humans can't see us the way that you can. The area has been shrouded in an illusion that protects us from prying eyes."

"What sort of illusion?"

"I'm sure you noticed how the ground glimmers when the sunlight hits it. It is that glow that makes us invisible, so that humans and their devices can't detect us."

"Then . . . what happens at night?"

"Well, we are miles away from the nearest house, so we don't have to worry too much about people finding us at night."

Ava nodded, still only half-understanding.

"So, this place is kind of a sanctuary for Acathodians?"

"More or less, yes. We still help a very small number of Acathodians who need to adapt to human life, but our main goal is to work with students around your age who have started to evolve."

"How many students are there?"

"Twelve new ones this year. Which is actually a higher number than usual. Altogether, we have about three hundred students and fourteen teachers, not including other staff members like our chief and custodian."

Ezra glanced at a huge clock hanging on the wall. "Wow, it's getting late. I must go make my rounds. Sorry to leave you, but you have a wonderful tour guide right next to you."

He gestured toward Sura.

"Oh, this will be fun, Ava," Sura said, eyes bright. "I can't wait to show you everything from the good old days when I used to live here!"

Ezra stood and bowed his head slightly. "I hope you ladies have a wonderful night. I will see you in the morning to walk Ava to her classes. Sura, Ava has your old room. The password never changed."

"A dream . . ." Sura called to Ezra as he began to walk off.

"Within a dream," he replied with a smile.

Ava huffed. "Well, that was cryptic. What does that mean?"

"It's just something that a few of us, including your father, said to each other before we went to bed," Sura said.

"My head is spinning with all these new surprises," she said, unable to keep the slight edge out of her tone. It felt like everyone knew more than she did, and she hated that.

"So, it's like 'good night,' or 'sweet dreams?'"

"Kind of. It's our way of saying we must live life to the fullest. Basically, start the day as if it was your last, and don't compare it to the past."

"I like that," Ava said.

Sura led Ava to the fifth floor, where they turned down a short hallway with rustic dark wood paneling on the walls. Ava began to gain a better understanding of what her mother had meant. In each nook and cranny, around every corner, everything had a story, a magical sense of wonder. She decided to pay close attention to every detail.

"Here we are," Sura said with a smile, her hand raised and showcasing the entrance.

They arrived at a door engraved with a familiar shield. Unlike the other doors, this one had no handle.

"Are you ready to see your room?" Sura asked, full of pride.

"I guess this is where the password comes in?"

"You bet, minnow. Shall I do the honors? Or would you like to try?"

"I'm good. Go for it, Mom."

Sura took Ava's hand. A shiver ran down her spine as an ancient and powerful language flowed from her mother's lips.

"Esh-my-eem."

The door opened. As she walked into the room, Ava noticed a wall stacked from floor to ceiling with books. The books surrounded the only window in the room, creating an ever-changing pattern, like a kaleidoscope of swirling patterns. Though they didn't have a shred of dust on them, the books seemed faded and old. The walls of the room were made of gray stone, sometimes interwoven with dark wood. A magnificent red and gold carpet lay on the floor in front of a small stone fireplace and opposite that was a bed. My bed, Ava thought with a small smile. All the furniture was made of brass and dark burnished wood.

"Wow, this room is amazing. I get to live here?" Ava was stunned.

"The room has not changed at all." Sura walked around, softly touching the fireplace, and scanning the books.

"So, this was your room? Mom, this is so cool!"

"For twelve years of my life . . . Jeez, that makes me feel old," Sura laughed. "We should get you settled. You have a big day tomorrow."

"Yeah, that's a good idea. Where is your room?"

"I have a room for the night, don't worry about me," Sura said, still staring at the things that were once her own.

"The night?" Ava questioned, realization slowly dawning.

This wasn't a move for her mother, it was a drop off.

"You're leaving me here?"

Sura smiled. "You can't expect me to go to school with you?"

"No, I know, but—" Her mother was the only thing she'd brought from her old life. She'd taken it for granted that she'd be with her. But that was silly. She was growing up. She needed to do this on her own. "I just . . . can't believe that I said goodbye to Kevin only this morning. And now I have to say goodbye to you. It's all happening so fast."

"Time is funny like that. Sometimes we want to stop it or slow it down—maybe even speed it up. But time will always go at its own speed," Sura mused. "Twenty minutes ago, this room didn't exist to you, and three hours ago, this building didn't exist to you. Two days ago, this entire world didn't exist to you. Imagine what wonders you will discover tomorrow, and the days after."

Ava smiled while she unpacked the last of her clothes and arranged the stuffed animals and swimming trophies she had brought from home neatly around the room.

"That looks better," she said. A smile came to her lips, but it was accompanied by the slightest pang of sadness. She still missed Kevin, and wondered what he was up to.

Sura put an arm around her daughter's shoulders and gave her a tight squeeze as they admired the room. "It looks perfect, Ava."

"Sweetheart, wake up," Sura said quietly. Ava rolled over to see that the sun had not yet fully risen.

"Mom?" Ava croaked, groggy-eyed. "It's so early . . . Can't I stay in bed for a couple more hours?"

"I know, I know, I'm sorry to wake you. But I need to show you something. Come quickly so we don't miss it!"

Sura led Ava out of her room and to the very end of the hallway, the dim lights guiding their way. They arrived at a winding staircase which led up to the roof.

"Here, wrap yourself in this, it's chilly out," Sura said, handing Ava a shawl.

"Mom what the heck are we doing up here? It's like, five AM."

"5:40, to be exact."

"Well, that's still early. You said we had a big day, and I need . . ."

Ava trailed off as the sun rose over the lake, lighting up the sky with all the colors this world had to offer. She gasped as she walked closer to the edge of the roof. A warm breeze filled the air, and in the distance, Ava saw birds circle the skies, singing to the new morning sun.

"Close your eyes. What are your senses telling you?"

Ava closed her eyes and took a deep breath. "I smell the lake and the trees. I hear the birds singing."

"Yes. Now focus on the birdsong," Sura directed.

Ava recognized the tune and began to hum along. She opened her eyes and looked at her mother.

"Mom . . . it's the lullaby you've been singing to me all these years." Ava fell into her mother's arms, hugging her tightly. "All this time, you were singing the song you heard here as a child."

"Every rough day, every sad moment, every time I just needed a break, I found myself here. Watching the sunrise and sunset. I sang along with the birds and realized that everything would be okay. This is also where I came up with the idea that life is a dream within a dream."

Ava's anticipation built as the warmth of the sun washed over her. A special new day was dawning. Sounds of students waking up and getting ready for the day emerged in the background. Though still hesitant, a new feeling started to creep into Ava's heart. Excitement.

8

First Day Jitters

"Mom, I'm still in my pajamas. I don't want to meet my classmates for the first time dressed in your hand-me-down t-shirt!"

"Well, we can't have that," Sura chuckled. "Let's get you back to your room."

Mother and daughter sprinted down the stairs, their laughs echoing through the hallway.

"Do you remember the password?" Sura asked as they approached the door. "It's your room now."

Ava looked up at her mother and smiled.

"Esh-my-eem," she said proudly. "Mom, quick question, can't anyone enter the room if they know the password? Like, maybe I shouldn't shout it out like a hotdog guy at a baseball game."

"You would think, but it seems there is magic behind the door, and it knows your voice and mine."

Ava's eyes widened. "Magic?"

"Well," she continued, running a brush through her long silver hair. "Let's get this day going. You have lots to do, friends to make, and a whole world to explore."

When Ava ran back to the room to get changed, she saw Ezra's shiny blue letter sticking out of her mother's purse. Ava quickly unfolded the letter.

My dear Sura,
You have been challenged like no other, and it pains me that you will have to endure even more hardship. This being said, you know what is at stake.
Once more, I ask you to be strong.
I promise to watch over Ava as if she were my own.
All my love,
Maridius

Ava re-read the letter, waiting for the words to sink in. But they simply couldn't. Her heart squeezed in her chest. What was at stake? It sounded dangerous. And with her mother leaving her, who would protect her?

In a daze, Ava slowly walked into the hall with the letter in hand.

"Mom?" she said quietly.

"I see you've found Maridius's letter . . ." Sura sighed and pressed her lips together.

Tears began to well up in Ava's eyes, spilling over onto her cheeks. "What does this mean?"

"You are a strong young woman, and I have every faith that you are ready to start this new adventure on your own. You're about to learn so much . . . You won't even notice I'm gone."

She shook her head, unable to believe it. "Who is Maridius? Have I met him before?"

"Maridius is the headmaster of the other school that I was telling you about—the underwater school of Hadal," Sura explained. "He is Enzo's grandson."

"I need breakfast," Ava said, refusing to think of it anymore. She was too upset and hungry to handle any more changes or surprises.

"Maybe I should just stop asking questions. It seems I never like the answers anyway."

"Just enjoy the ride. Let's go see how the dining hall can spoil us today," Sura chirped, visibly relieved that Ava was done asking questions.

They spotted Ezra on their way downstairs.

"Good morning, ladies," he said. "I gather you slept well?"

"Good morning, Ezra," Ava replied. "I slept great, thanks."

"I'm happy to see you two in such good spirits," Ezra said, glancing over his shoulder ever so briefly.

"Oh, I know that look . . ." Sura smirked. "A tough new family, huh?"

"I try to refrain from talking about other students in front of their peers—" He lowered his voice, "but this kid has quite an attitude."

"Well, I guess we'd better let you go handle that," Sura said. "Ava and I are going to get a bite to eat. Have fun." She hugged Ezra briefly before they parted ways.

"Thanks for the pity hug . . . Or an understanding hug? Not sure which you were going for."

"Sounds like you could use both," Sura said with a laugh.

Ava and Sura were greeted with a sweet, fishy scent as they entered the dining hall. The sounds of students' conversations ran up and down the long wooden tables. Ava blinked, overwhelmed by the sheer number of students. Ezra had said there were around 300, but it sure seemed like more. Many of them looked like her. Not the pale young woman with mousy brown locks, but the new her, with purple hair, bright orange eyes, and a longing for seafood unlike any other.

Ava grabbed a tray and approached the buffet. She feasted her eyes on lox, white fish, lobster soup, eggs, fruit, caviar, and a wide range of sushi. She took as much as she could carry—at least two of everything—and a tower of sushi that teetered precariously on her plate. Ava carried her over-filled dish back to her mother's table, as carefully as if she were walking on a tightrope.

"Thanks, hon," Sura said, stealing a few pieces of sushi.

"No problem." Ava softly set the plate down.

"How are you feeling?"

"Honestly? Scared, nervous, excited. Maybe a little sad." Ava's lower lip had a slight quiver. Sadness was definitely at the forefront of all other emotions.

"Sounds like a good mix of emotions," Sura said to console Ava.

"So, are you leaving today?" Ava asked. Her tone was sharper than she intended.

"Yes, dear, I need to. I have work to do at home. Plus, you need to start meeting people and having fun without me. I may be a cool mom, but . . ." She scanned the room. "I'm not nearly as cool as the students here."

"This place is just so big! I feel lost. What happens if I can't make friends?"

Sura gently took Ava's hand. "Ava, sometimes we might struggle to understand the world around us. But that doesn't mean we won't find a home, no matter where we are. You have always had an ability to connect with people. Now you get to connect with people who will truly understand you. I have so much faith in you! Now it's time to have faith in yourself."

With that, Sura grabbed her plate and walked over for another helping of food. "It's also a *really* fun process," she called over her shoulder. "You'll see what I mean."

Ava looked around the dining hall, still stunned by the beauty of the place. The rustic stone, brick, and wood that decorated the room was breathtaking. There were paintings on the walls that could easily have been showcased in the world's finest museums.

"Ladies!" called a voice.

Ava turned her head to see Ezra walking their way.

"What a glorious day!" Ezra sat down. "We have fun times ahead of us, Ava."

She wanted to smile, but her nerves took over. There was so much to learn. Sura sat back down with a fresh heap of fruit.

"Nervous, I see?" Ezra said.

"We're feeling some jitters today," Sura confirmed, tracing a soothing circle on Ava's back. "But our girl is strong."

Ava rolled her eyes. She felt as if she was back in first grade, afraid to walk through the door. The image of her teacher crouched awkwardly and trying to cheer her on came to mind. Maybe Ava did need to woman-up a bit. She wiggled her body indicating her mother needed to remove her hand from her back.

Sura smiled and got the hint and went back to eating her food.

When they had eaten to their hearts' content, Ava, Sura, and Ezra all got up and made their way out of the dining hall. At every table they passed, at least one student reached out to high five or fist bump Ezra.

"He's always been Mr. Popular," Sura quipped.

"I can't help it; people just love me!" Ezra said with a dramatic shrug.

"Ezra, Ezra!" a student called out as he ran up to them.

"Carl! What's up, pal?"

"I don't want to interrupt you, but no one is answering my emails. I *know* what I saw . . . I'm not crazy. You gotta believe that!" Carl sounded deeply agitated.

Ava gave her mother a look.

"Carl, meet Ava," Ezra said.

"Oh . . . Sorry. Hi, Ava."

"Hi . . ." Ava replied hesitantly.

She was preoccupied with Carl's appearance. Ava hadn't even begun to get used to her own changes so Ava did what anyone would do. She gawked at Carl. He was tall and had dark, scaly skin with hints of yellow. If he was a snake, you'd immediately know that he was venomous. His red-flecked orange eyes made his pupils look like they were on fire.

Ezra's voice interrupted her thoughts. "Carl, this is not the best time. Can we talk about this later? I have to show Ava to her classes."

"Yeah, sure. Sorry. But I'm telling you—" Carl started again.

"I know, and I hear you. I just can't talk now," Ezra said in a calm and understanding tone, holding his palms up.

Carl looked around before meeting Ava's curious gaze.

"It was nice meeting you, Ava. If you ever need anything, please feel free to ask," Carl said, ignoring Ava's gawking.

"Sorry, nice meeting you as well, Carl," Ava said with a smile of embarrassment.

Once they reached the main lobby, Ezra stopped. It was then that Ava realized she needed to say goodbye to her mom.

"I think it's time for me to leave you to your own adventures. You're going to be great here, Ava." Noticing Ava's stiffness, Sura drew her daughter into a tight hug.

"I don't want you to go," Ava whispered in her mother's ear.

"Trust me, you'll be fine. You need to explore, learn, and grow. Once you get settled in here, you won't even notice I'm gone. I'm so excited for you!"

Ava was filled once again with the urge to scream, making her realize that her childhood home was still out there. A feeling of calmness and rationality washed over Ava, giving her a moment to take a deep, comforting breath. The fear dissipated, for now.

Sura glanced at Ezra with a warm smile.

"Ezra is like family. If you need anything, he will always be here for you."

With that, Ezra placed a comforting hand on Ava's shoulder and waved Sura away." I will make sure that she is safe. Now it's time for you to go. We've got a busy day ahead."

Sura nodded and walked out the massive door, turning to catch Ava's eye one last time before it closed behind her. After a moment, Ezra broke the silence. "Well . . . we've got more important things to do than stare at the door all day. What do you say?"

Ava couldn't help but laugh as he set off down the hallway.

"Ava, I know this was all just thrown at you, so let me offer you a gift via a story. Did you ever hear about the time when your father, mother, and I all rode on the back of a whale shark?"

"Umm, no. Please share."

Ezra cleared his throat and began his story.

"Well, your father was a real risk taker, but your mother only made him more daring. One day, we were all swimming deep in the ocean and we saw the most beautiful whale shark." He paused to make sure she was following him as they took a sharp left turn down another hallway.

"Your mother started to swim next to it, and your father and I followed. Now, these things are huge, so of course your father made it his mission to ride on the whale shark's back. Whale sharks are mostly harmless, but they really don't like being touched. After a few minutes of writhing and trying to throw him off, the shark finally gave in and let him come along for a ride. Your mother and I climbed aboard, and we rode for about three hundred yards until the whale shark decided it had had enough."

"That's *amazing*!" Ava exclaimed.

Ezra laughed. "If you think that's amazing just wait until you have your own stories to tell."

They kept on walking through the maze of hallways, and soon Ava had no idea where they were. Around every turn, historical artifacts lined the walls. Ezra pointed out a few, many of them ornate weapons.

Despite being hundreds of years old, they looked sharp and polished, as though they could be used today.

They walked into a small office, and Ezra approached the front desk. Behind the desk sat a woman whose face resembled that of a blowfish. Her eyes sparkled as she caught sight of Ezra.

"Hi Tetra! Hope you're doing well today," Ezra said, flashing a smile. "Ava Greene, please."

Tetra's scales brightened. She dug around in a file cabinet and handed him a small envelope.

"This," Ezra said as he gave Ava the envelope, "is your class schedule. Have a look."

* *First Period — History — 9am - 10:45 am*
* *Second Period — Self-Defense — 11am - 12:45pm*
* *Lunch — 1pm - 3pm*
* *Third Period — Underwater Training - 3:15pm - 5pm*

"What do you think, Ava?"

"This looks amazing. But why self-defense?" Ava asked, a chill creeping down her spine.

Ezra paused before replying. "The world is a dark and dangerous place, Ava. Why not know how to defend yourself?"

Ava didn't argue. She wasn't new to learning martial arts; she'd studied krav maga for two years back home. She wasn't completely naive either, she knew the world wasn't all sunshine and rainbows. But Ava had the feeling Ezra wasn't talking about the dangers she saw on the news at night. Ezra was talking about a danger far worse than that, one not found on the local news but in the world of horror films. This world was so different than the one she once knew. Ava tried not to spiral down the path of fear, but to see it as an adventure.

They approached a room where Ava could hear a group of kids singing. Their voices sounded ethereal; there was something magical about how the harmonies played off one another.

"I know they're wonderful, but if we don't keep moving, we'll never make it to your class. They have a way of mesmerizing people."

"Good idea," Ava said as they continued to walk down the hall. "I could feel myself getting lured in by their voices. That was so strange."

"I'm sure you've heard of the Siren song," Ezra replied, which made her eyes widen. Those were sirens? They were real. Before she could ask, he stopped in front of a door. "Ah, and here we are! Your first class: History with Professor Lundlow. Head on in, Lundlow is expecting you. I'll be in my office if you need me."

"Thanks, Ezra."

Ava took a deep breath and opened the arched wooden door. A strange looking man stood on a table in the front of the room, eyes looking upon Ava. Lundlow's skin was almost transparent. If it weren't for the bluish white outline of his body and the swirling light blue dust that filled him in, she wouldn't have been able to see him.

"Why, hello, you must be Ava," Lundlow said in a twangy voice.

"Yes, sir," Ava replied hesitantly.

"No need to be shy. Go ahead and take a seat."

As Ava walked to the back of the classroom, she made eye contact with her fellow classmates. Some of the students were almost fully evolved, while others still looked more or less human.

One student looked like he was at the awkward pubescent stage of evolution. One eye was clearly more Acathodian—big and round with splashes of bright green—while his other eye was still small and beady. His teeth protruded out from unexpectedly large lips, and his skin had a light pink tint that made him look flushed and sickly.

To her left, Ava noticed a girl who looked familiar. It was strange to recognize anyone in such a place. Ava's eyes fixated on the girl who donned long red hair with blonde highlights and large purple eyes. The girl shot Ava with a nasty look.

Ava quickly redirected her gaze onto the old paintings, tools, and weapons that embellished the gray brick walls of the classroom. Ava found her seat. The seats were more like cozy living room recliners than typical, stiff classroom desks. She could get used to this.

Still standing on his desk, Professor Lundlow began his lecture.

"Alright class, quiet down." Lundlow cleared his throat. "You all know that I love to have fun."

The students exchanged glances, mildly perplexed.

"Yes! Remember that time when we threw eggs at each other? Or that time we made slime that turned our skin green for a week?"

The class acknowledged Lundlow's words with smiles and laughs.

"Well, unfortunately, today won't be a fun day. History is sometimes a dreadful thing, and we have some serious material to cover. It is important to learn about our enemies, both in the past, and those who are still a threat today."

Nervous murmurs filled the room.

Lundlow continued. "Has anyone ever heard of a bunyip before? What about grindylows?"

Everyone in the class seemed puzzled except for the girl with the red hair. She had her arm elegantly stretched upward with her index finger raised.

"Yes, Natalie?" Lundlow called.

Ava jolted, repeating the name twice in her head to connect where she'd heard that name before.

Then, like a punch in the gut, the realization hit her. She was the girl Ava swam against at the Indiana state championships!

Ava gaped. She was grateful to see a familiar face, but not if it was going to stare daggers her way.

Is she mad because I beat her? Ava thought. *Maybe that's just how she is all the time.*

Either way, she didn't want to pass up a conversation with someone she knew. Maybe Natalie wasn't the most desirable link to her past life, but comfort was needed right now, even with an attitude. Her attention went back to Professor Lundlow's lesson.

Natalie began to answer the question, each word perfectly pronounced. "A bunyip, or bunny-ips as my mother and I like to call them, are like sea dogs. If you train them properly, they're as harmless as puppies."

"I'm afraid you're mistaken," Lundlow responded. "Bunyips have razor-sharp teeth and are quite deadly. They have been hunting our kind for thousands of years. Bunyips are only loyal to those who have evil hearts, so they could never be tamed by one of us."

"I don't know about that," one student murmured. "Natalie seems pretty evil to me."

Lundlow shot a warning look at the boy who made the comment. "Usually, bunyips hunt in packs—much like wolves. When you fight one, you fight them all. Their name literally means 'devil,' or 'evil spirit.' This creature hails from Aboriginal Australia and is known to lurk in swamps, creeks, and riverbeds. Aborigines believed bunyips resorted to eating humans when their food source was disturbed. They have flippers, tusks, a horse-like tail, and teeth that can bite through pretty much anything. Their cries are bone-chilling and are heard most clearly in the dead of night."

All eyes in the class turned to Natalie, who didn't look the slightest bit defeated. She scoffed at Lundlow and then looked around the room, daring her classmates to say something.

"What about grindylows?" Lundlow continued.

This time Natalie simply folded her arms.

A boy with golden spikes coming out of his head tentatively raised his hand. Ava recognized him from the dining hall.

"Go ahead, Naveen."

"My parents used to tell me stories of grindylows to scare me so I wouldn't go swimming alone. They said that grindylows have red eyes and long sharp fingers that they use to drag children into the lake and other cold, dark bodies of water."

"Very good!" Lundlow's swirling blue insides seemed to glow a bit brighter. "Unfortunately, these creatures aren't imaginary, they exist in the real world. Grindylows are extremely deadly. These water demons were first mentioned in British folklore and can be traced back to the region of Yorkshire. They are about five feet tall with green scaly skin, and they smell horrible. Though you would think their scent could help prevent sneak attacks, they move extremely quickly. Even if you smell them coming, you rarely have time to prepare yourself."

Ava blinked. *Do I need to fight monsters? Seriously? Was this the danger Ezra was speaking about?*

Even as Lundlow moved on, Ava kept coming back to that single word: *Monsters*. The thought of them lurking below the surface of the sea had her rooted to her seat, her body frozen with terror. It was a feeling Ava had never felt before.

A gong rang throughout the hall and students started packing up their belongings. Ava eagerly followed suit, happy to end this nightmare of a class.

As they left, Lundlow spoke over the ding. "Class, please know that you do not need to worry about these creatures just yet. You are all safe on land, and especially at this school. When you learn how to defend yourselves, these beasts won't seem as scary. If you have any other questions, I will be in my office after lunch."

Ava rushed over to Natalie, who was busy packing up her things.

"Hi, your name is Natalie, right? We swam together at the—"

"Yes, I know you," the girl interrupted. "So what?"

Caught off guard by the girl's rude response, Ava fumbled for words. "Oh . . . well . . . I just thought it would be nice to get to know each other, seeing as—"

"Why? Because we raced once?"

Ava stared, unsure how to respond.

"Umm, yes. Exactly that, actually." Ava decided to address the elephant in the room. "I'm sorry, but what's your problem with me?"

She snorted. "I would watch your back if I were you." She stormed past Ava, leaving her stunned.

A much friendlier-looking classmate came to Ava's rescue. The girl had bright blue hair and hazel eyes that sat quite far apart on her face.

"Hi there! Don't take her too seriously, she just got here and thinks she runs the school already. I'm Harper." She stuck out her hand for a shake.

"Hey, I'm Ava. What's her deal?"

"I don't really know. She's only been here for one day and is already making all kinds of 'friends.'"

"Huh . . . I know her from back home. We swam against each other at a state championship."

"I hope you won!" Harper said.

"Don't worry, I did!"

"Good, you're my hero," Harper stated with a laugh.

"So, by any chance, do you know where the self-defense class is?"

"I'll take you; I have that class next, too," Harper said, pointing the direction.

"Thank you. Hopefully one day I will know where I am going around here."

"Don't worry, you will," Harper said.

9

Knives Out

As they approached their self-defense class, Ava could hear the muffled clangs of weapons clashing behind the door. When Harper and Ava entered, they were swept into a flurry of shuffling feet and thunderous shouts. They quickly made their way to safety in a distant corner of the room lined with racks of swords, knives, clubs, hammers, shields, axes, and spears.

As Ava looked around the room, tracing the sharp, jagged blades with her eyes, one thing seemed obvious: she would absolutely need to fight monsters.

Harper pointed out the large circle of Acathodians that had gathered around two fighters in the middle of the room. Ava moved closer to the circle so she could see the fight. Two tall students were at the center of the action. Both wore helmets, but one was armed with a wooden spear while the other held a long wooden knife. One fierce blow after another, their weapons clashed and slammed down on each other's armor. Suddenly, the student with the long knife spun under her opponent's spear and landed a stunning blow with the hilt of her knife, knocking the other student down. The spear-wielder raised his hands, and the match was over.

“I could have used some of these skills growing up in the Bronx,” Harper said, laughing.

“Very well done, Victoria and Leon,” a voice congratulated.

The fighters shook hands.

“*Rok Kazock*!” Both fighters said in unison.

“Raw ka-what? What does that mean?” Ava asked quietly.

“*Rok Kazock*,” Harper corrected. “That’s our battle cry. It means . . . Hmm . . . I guess the best translation is: ‘Don’t mess with us!’ You can also think of it like, ‘Let’s shoot the thirty.’”

“What does ‘shoot the thirty’ mean?”

Harper laughed. “Never mind. I’ll teach you some of my hometown slang one day.”

The next two students entered the combat circle. One student wore freshly polished black armor and held a blue metal sword and shield. The other student had dual axes and was dressed in silver armor. Harper pulled Ava along as she pushed and twisted her way into the inner circle.

“Trust me, you’ll want to see this up close,” Harper said with an excited smile.

As Ava and Harper made it deeper into the circle, she saw two students taunting one another with sharp-bladed weapons. “Are those real weapons? Shouldn’t we get a teacher to stop them?”

“Do you see that woman with short blonde hair? Cheering on the fighters? That’s Agatha, the teacher.” Harper said with a smile and quick laugh.

Ava paused, trying to comprehend this new life of hers. Back home self-defense class was a punching bag and learning how to kick. Here it was blades and a teacher directing you to kill one another.

“This is not to the death, is it?” Ava asked, speaking loudly to be heard over the other students’ chants.

Harper looked over her shoulder. “Don’t be ridiculous, Ava. They are best friends.”

“What if they get hurt?” Ava’s voice cracked with concern.

"Don't worry, the school has potions that can heal almost anything."

Ava stared at her new friend. Healing potions? What kind of world was this? But Ava quickly lost the thought as the fight began.

The students stood tall with their chests puffed out, silently glaring into each other's eyes. Agatha's sword made a slicing sound as she freed it from its sheath. Ava felt a cool whoosh of breeze when she swept it through the air in a downward motion.

The student with the axes attempted a series of consecutive strikes, his weapons swinging one after the other. The fighter in black ducked and dodged, blocking the more accurate hits with his shield. The students cheered the fighters on. It seemed to Ava that this was a one-sided fight. The student with the axes was definitely winning. The fighter with the sword and shield was blocking and moving a lot, but had not made a single strike.

Suddenly, the tables turned. The fighter with the black armor deflected both axes with his shield, knocking the student in silver off balance. The student in black then launched toward his opponent, using his shield in a brutal attack to knock him down. As he began to rise to his feet, the fighter in black spun around behind the student in silver, landing another vicious blow with his shield. The fighter fell to the ground once again, but quickly braced himself and rolled out of the way of another shield attack. Visibly enraged, he prepared to attack. He wielded his dual axes in powerful strokes, but only managed to knock his opponent slightly off balance.

Ava counted six ax strikes, but each blow was blocked by the other fighter's shield. She noticed though that the student in silver was starting to tire—he was slumped over as though he had been hit in the gut.

"The guy with the shield hasn't attacked more than twice, but it looks like he's winning," Ava said to Harper.

"Oh, you have no idea how much he's holding back. That's Joshua Briggs. He has a reputation for being the best fighter in the whole school."

Just then, the silver fighter aimed one last strike at Joshua's neck. The class gasped. Joshua moved back just in time and drew his sword, cutting through the air in a blur of bluish steel. He narrowly missed his opponent. The two students faced each other and regained their composure.

The student in silver charged Joshua, but with one simple step he moved out of the way and countered with a powerful shield strike. The other fighter leapt off the ground and let out a powerful war cry. Before the crazed student in silver could reach him, Joshua attacked with four mighty strikes, sending the silver-cladded fighter to the ground. Joshua roared as he raised his sword high in the air. In a flash, he brought his blade down in a stabbing motion, stopping about an inch away from the other student's neck.

The students cheered as the student in silver raised his hands in surrender. Joshua backed away, put his sword in its sheath, and helped the defeated fighter up to his feet. The boys shook hands and clapped each other on the back. After they released their embrace, Joshua started to celebrate with his classmates. When he took off his helmet, he shook his dark brown hair out of his face. Ava was captured by his strong jaw and sparkling gray eyes. He had a wonderful smile.

"Oh yeah, and I forgot to add. . . He's gorgeous!" Harper fanned her face in imitation of the puppy-eyed girls that surrounded him.

Ava laughed awkwardly but nodded in agreement.

Agatha congratulated the fighters. "Good job, Hathor, very strong and aggressive! Next time, save that energy and use it in the final blows of the combat."

Hathor nodded before turning to his opponent. "I'll get you next time, Josh."

"Sure you will, buddy," Joshua laughed and brought Hathor in for a brotherly hug.

The students fanned out into the room, and the hubbub of clangs and shouts once again filled the air.

Agatha caught sight of Ava and Harper and walked over. "You must be Ava. It's a pleasure to meet you. Wow, what a beautiful necklace you have."

Ava touched the pendant. "Thank you, Agatha. Or do I call you Mrs.—"

Agatha cut her off, still gazing in wonder at the necklace. "Agatha is fine."

"My mother gave me this necklace before we came here. I know it's silly, but for some reason it makes me feel like I can do anything."

"Hmmm, very interesting," Agatha said, bending closer to observe the pendant.

Then she quickly straightened up. "Alrighty then, let's see what you can do."

They walked to the wall that was covered with clubs and barbed poles.

"These look dangerous," Ava said.

"They are, in fact, quite deadly. Now, pick one up and let's test it out," Agatha commanded.

Wide-eyed, Ava looked at the wall of weapons and then back at Agatha. "I've never used a weapon before."

"You'll have to figure out your weapon of choice eventually. No time like the present to give it a go."

Ava hesitantly reached for a red-tinted metal club that had a large orb fixed on the top. A dim blue light seemed to shine from inside the sphere.

"It's pretty heavy, but I like this one," Ava stated, turning the weapon in her hands.

"Interesting choice," Agatha said. "That is called a Morning Star. Follow me."

Agatha walked back to the center of the room. Ava followed, dragging the Morning Star along behind her. A few of the other students noticed and started snickering. Agatha quickly turned around to see Ava a few feet away, struggling with the weapon as if it were an anvil.

As Ava approached, she could see that her teacher was trying not to smile as well.

"Pick it up and get ready," Agatha stated in a stern voice.

Ava had to use her entire body to lift her weapon. It wobbled in her hands as she tried to steady her stance.

"*Bapalo*!" Agatha screamed, making Ava jump. For such a small person, she had strong lungs.

A half wooden, half metallic training dummy popped out from one of the walls. The automaton was coming right for Ava. She quickly started to walk backward toward Agatha.

"There is no running away, Ava. This thing will kill you," Agatha said.

"Kill me? What kind of school is this?" Ava cried.

"You need to fight."

Ava frowned as a few students laughed harder. She did not like that one bit, but she had a more pressing problem. The dummy was creeping up on her. She stopped, planted her feet, and lifted the Morning Star high. The wooden attacker suddenly sped toward her and Ava swung her weapon with all her might. A burst of light flashed out from the bluish orb, knocking Ava off her feet.

"Ha! It's got quite the kick, doesn't it?" Agatha shouted with a fierce smile.

Ava scrambled up off the floor. "What was that?"

"Kickback," Agatha explained. "These training weapons are designed to add an impact force to simulate real battle."

"How did I do?"

Agatha laughed. "Not great. You shouldn't end your fight on the floor. I know you've had no training, but when you find your weapon, it should instinctively feel right. There are many more to try. Follow me."

Agatha led Ava to the weapon wall once again. Ava steered away from the heavier weapons and looked for something that she could control. She grasped a pair of hand axes.

"Are you ready?" Agatha said.

Ava held each ax tightly and braced herself.

"Ready!" she shouted.

"*Bapalo*!" Agatha screamed once more.

The attack dummy's eyes lit up and focused on its target. Ava took a deep breath and fought the urge to run away again. Instead, she took a leap to the side of the dummy and struck its shoulder. The dummy wobbled back. Ava grinned at Agatha with pride—she couldn't believe she had actually hit it! But the fight was not over yet. Ava turned just in time to see the dummy rushing at her.

Ava stumbled backward but the dummy struck, knocking her to the ground. She quickly got up and attacked her assailant head-on. She struck the dummy's head, but the impact of the blow knocked the ax out of her hand. Though Ava was caught off guard, she used the other ax to hit the dummy's torso. Once again, the ax bounced out of Ava's hand and went flying past Agatha's head. The dummy swung at Ava one last time, knocking her forcefully to the ground. She felt the wind leave her lungs all at once and gasped for air, clutching her stomach.

"*La'atsor*!" Agatha screamed, bringing the dummy to a sudden halt.

Ava remained on the floor, defeated. She wasn't terribly hurt, but her cheeks burned from embarrassment and anger.

"Damn! I thought I had it!"

"You almost did, but you let your guard down," Agatha said, crouching beside her. "I don't think the ax is right for you, either."

"Really? I thought I did well."

Agatha glanced at the wall that had one of Ava's axes planted in it. "We're getting there, but you're definitely not an ax fighter."

Ava followed her gaze and laughed. "I guess not."

"Up we go," Agatha said.

The next wall was full of knives.

"Okay," Ava said. "I can get with this."

Ava was drawn to a grouping of blue metal knives that were about six inches long. The knives were thin and looked incredibly sharp. Ava grabbed three knives in one hand, two in the other, and made her way back toward the training dummy. This time, she was resolved to win.

Agatha followed her to the sparring station, smiling as she saw the determination on Ava's face. Before Agatha could even ask, Ava moved into a fighting stance.

"Ready!" she shouted forcefully.

The tension in the air was thick. Everyone in the room was focused on Ava. Ignoring the stares, Ava clenched her teeth and concentrated solely on defeating the attack dummy.

"*Bapalo*!"

Once again, the blue eyes gleamed to life and the attack dummy launched forward. Ava thrust her body in the opposite direction and ran from the dummy. Most of the class started to laugh. Joshua, however, took an interest and stepped forward.

Ava suddenly stopped and twisted toward the dummy, throwing her first knife. It planted itself firmly in the dummy's chest. The class was shocked into silence. The next knife she threw also hit its target, landing only an inch away from the first.

"*Yes*!" Agatha shouted.

The dummy was beginning to slow down, but it continued to wobble closer to Ava. Without hesitation, Ava flung another knife into her attacker's chest, lodging it right below the last. Ava's necklace started to glow as she leapt and spun away from the dummy. Gaining more force, she threw one more blade, striking the dummy right between the eyes. Once Ava landed gracefully back on her feet, she rushed at the dummy, sharp blade in hand, and soared into the air. She struck her last knife into the dummy's head, and it went crashing to the floor.

Ava was caught up in the whoosh of exhilaration that swept over her. Harper began to applaud, and the rest of the class followed suit, erupting into hoots and hollers.

"I think we've found your weapon," Agatha said.

"I'm not even sure how I did that!" Ava said, slightly out of breath.

"Your skill with knives must come from your mother. That's why you felt so comfortable with them. Even though you did well, there is much more for you to learn."

"My mother?" Ava was still beaming.

Agatha bent down slightly and smiled at Ava. "The apple never falls that far from the tree, does it?"

10

Testing the Waters

Ava stood tall, smiling at her victory. Harper rushed over to Ava. "That was amazing! Was that really your first time fighting with knives?"

"That felt unbelievable, I didn't know I had that in me."

Just then, Joshua and Hathor brushed by them. As they passed, Joshua met Ava's gaze for a few seconds, a smile tugging at one corner of his lips.

"Ava, did you see that?" Harper whispered.

"See what?" Ava responded, feigning ignorance.

"Okay, suuure. Like he wasn't totally ogling you. Anyway, I want to show you something before we head to lunch. Follow me."

Ava and Harper jogged down the hall to a door made of petrified wood. Black metal links decorated the hinges.

"This is my favorite place in the entire school," Harper said.

She opened the door to reveal a massive library. The majestic bookshelves rose almost forty feet into the air, leading to an incredible stained-glass ceiling. The radiating fall colors gave the room an extra sense of calm. An old white willow tree stood tall in the center of the library, casting a shadow over two rustic wood benches, each decorated with colorful pillows. As Ava walked in further, she noticed two wooden spiral staircases that twisted up to the second level of the library. She could already tell that this was going to be another one of her favorite places.

"Isn't it cool?" Harper asked, snapping her out of her mesmerized state.

"It's amazing!"

"Alright, we should go eat lunch before our next class. We'll need the fuel, trust me."

It was hard for Ava to leave the library, but she was hungry and couldn't wait to swim in the beautiful pool that Ezra had shown her the night before. By the time she and Harper made their way into the dining hall, it was already buzzing with students. The girls split off to opposite ends of the buffet and piled their plates high with food. They met back at a table in the middle of the hall. Ava and Harper quickly started devouring their lunches as they did not want to be late for class. When Ava finally finished her last piece of salmon, she looked up and took in her surroundings. She couldn't believe how at home she felt after just half a day of classes. That's when she noticed Joshua sitting at the table next to them with Hathor and a few other students from her Self-Defense class. She sat up straighter, fixed her hair, and ran her tongue over her teeth to make sure nothing was stuck in them.

"Ava, you should talk to him instead of primping for him," Harper giggled.

"What?!" Ava snapped. "I just—I'm not primping for anyone. I just wanted to . . . I have a boyfriend back home, you know."

"Sheesh, no need to be defensive!" Harper quipped, shoving another bite of food into her mouth. "He can still be fun to look at, even if you're not trying to date him."

Ava sighed. "I suppose . . ."

"So, tell me about this boyfriend."

"His name is Kevin. We've been together for about two years . . ." Ava stopped abruptly as her throat began to tighten. She swallowed her desire to cry and quickly changed the subject. "What about you, Harper? What's your story?"

"I'm a New Yorker, born and raised. I love fashion and long walks on the beach . . ."

Ava laughed. "Nice dating profile. How did you find yourself here?"

Harper took another bite of her food and shook her head slightly.

"You know, people called me a freak, weird, all kinds of names . . ."

"Because you were turning?" Ava asked.

"No, because I have eight toes on one foot."

"You have eight toes?! Let me see!" Ava blurted with excitement.

Harper laughed so hard that she spit up some water. "Oh, my lord, Ava, I was joking! You are so gullible!"

"Oh . . . I wonder why." Ava looked pointedly at a student with long gold spikes coming out of his head. "I either believe anything or nothing at all these days. I can't decide which one is best. But can you blame me?"

Harper followed her gaze and shrugged. "Yeah, good point."

"So, tell me more about yourself, I don't even know your last name?" Ava asked.

"Watson. I got here about six months ago and, like the majority of everyone else here, it was because I was starting to change. It was hard to leave my school, friends, and family but . . . You know how it is. Leave or die."

"Yeah, I know that feeling. What are you looking at?" Ava asked, suddenly aware that Harper was smirking at something going on behind her.

She turned her head trying to follow Harper's gaze. Joshua was approaching their table. Ava quickly jerked her head back toward Harper, with wide eyes.

"Is he coming over to us?"

Before Harper had time to answer, Joshua reached the edge of their table. Ava stiffened, refusing to look up as he said, "Hey, can I join you ladies?"

"Be our guest," Harper said.

She moved over to give him room to sit next to her, directly across from Ava. Harper winked at Ava when Joshua wasn't looking.

"H-hi . . ." Ava stuttered with bright red cheeks.

"Josh . . ." Harper chimed in, saving Ava from yelling something in gibberish. "Meet my new friend, Ava. She just got here yesterday. What's going on with you?"

"Oh, you know, same stuff as always," Joshua said dismissively. "It's nice to meet you, Ava. You really showed that dummy who was boss today."

Ava laughed nervously. "Thanks. You weren't too shabby yourself."

"Thank you," Joshua replied with a handsome, effortless grin. "So, tell me, how's your first day going?"

"This place is spectacular! Harper just took me to the library, which was magnificent, but when I saw the pool for the first time yesterday, I couldn't even speak. I've never seen anything like that before. I mean, every room in this school is just so beautiful," Ava gushed.

"I know what you mean. When I saw the library for the first time, I don't think I left for a week." Joshua leaned back in his chair, looking around like a king surveying his kingdom. "What did you like best?"

Ava smiled. "The bench under the white willow tree was definitely calling my name."

"So, you saw the library, the pool hall, the training room, and of course the dining hall. Anything else?" Joshua asked.

"Well, I had a class with Lundlow . . . and obviously I saw my room, if that counts?"

"It absolutely does. Maybe tomorrow I can show you more of the campus?" Joshua asked with a coolness Ava struggled to mirror.

"I . . . um . . . I would really like that." Ava did her best to quash nervousness bubbling up inside her. She didn't have a right to be feeling that way. Not after Kevin.

Then she noticed that kids were clearing their tables and beginning to leave the dining hall. She nudged Harper under the table.

"Oh, we need to go! Class starts in five minutes," Harper said as she quickly got up and grabbed her things.

Ava jerked out of her seat as well.

"Bye Josh." Harper winked at him as she slid off the bench.

"Catch you later, Harp! See you tomorrow, Ava. Meet me in the lobby at 5 PM?"

"Yeah. Sure. See you then," Ava called as Harper dragged her away by the crook of her elbow.

"Look at you. Your first day, and you already have a date with the hottest guy in school. Also, we might be late for class," Harper laughed as the girls exited the dining hall arm-in-arm.

"It's not a date, and how long do we have?" Ava stated with conviction as she picked up her pace.

"Run-o'clock," Harper said as both girls started to sprint.

"Ready?" Harper asked when they arrived at the door to the Pool Hall.

"Oh yeah, let's do this!" Ava said, still catching her breath.

Harper opened the door and Ava instantly got chills. It was as if the room had been crafted with magic.

As she took in her surroundings, Ava saw the other students starting to file in with their bathing suits on. The swimsuits were unlike any Ava had ever seen—and she had seen a ton. They looked a little like the classic one-piece that Ava had to wear when she swam in her swim meets, but these suits meshed so well with the bodies that they seemed to be a continuation of the swimmers' skin.

"I don't have a suit," Ava said.

"There's Professor Yara," Harper said, indicating a beautiful woman with a strong slender frame. "She can help you out."

Ava eyed her new professor as she approached. Yara's skin looked as if she was covered from head to toe with intricate, light pink markings. Yara was tall and beautiful with long, metallic pink hair, and light hazel eyes.

When Yara got within five feet of Ava, she opened her arms wide as if she expected a hug. Her dazzling hazel eyes pierced right through Ava, and she couldn't shake the feeling that she had met her before.

"Ava, it's so nice to see you all grown up!" Yara said, drawing Ava into her arms. When she let go, her hands remained on Ava's shoulders, and she took in every feature of her face. "My name is Yara. We haven't formally met, but I used to be very good friends with your mom. I was so happy to see her when she dropped you off."

"It is very nice to meet you," Ava said, a little embarrassed.

"I'm sure your mom never told you about me . . . Kind of hard to bring up this world in a casual conversation, right?"

"Yeah, I would say so!"

"Let's get to it. Harper, please direct Ava to the changing room. Ava, your swimsuit is in your locker. It will be a bit big, but once you're in the water, it will shrink to a perfect fit. Okay, go about it." Yara shooed them off in a playful way.

Ava and Harper made their way to the changing rooms at the back end of the pool hall. Harper led the way to her locker, and Ava found a blue and silver swimsuit neatly folded and ready for her to put on. Both girls changed as quickly as possible. Ava didn't want to waste another second.

"Interesting, the swimsuit is so flexible. I mean, it's a bit big like Yara said, but it's so comfortable." Ava rolled her shoulders to feel the fabric move with her body.

"Yeah, it's made from some super high-tech material and it's super comfortable," Harper said.

The smallest of ridges ran throughout the suit. Ava assumed that these were supposed to lessen resistance and help her glide in the water.

"Ready?" Ava was itching to get to the pool.

"Yep, let's go!" Harper answered.

The girls set off immediately to find Yara.

"Harper, Ava, you ladies ready?" Yara said from the side of the pool. "Go on!"

The girls exchanged smiles and then jumped in together. The water felt amazing on Ava's skin. Her hair flowed and danced around her. The last few days had been unsteady and confusing, but in this moment everything felt right. Ava opened her eyes as she twisted and spun through the water. She could see perfectly. She swam upward to pop her head out of the water.

"Feels marvelous, right?" Yara called.

Ava grinned back at her. There were no words to describe how great it felt. As Ava swam, the suit molded to her body, fitting snug on her skin.

"Okay, class! Let's start our lesson for today," Yara announced, clapping her hands to corral her students. Though Ava was underwater, she could hear Yara's voice. The words were faint, but the tone was all Ava needed. It was time to start class.

The splashing and laughing died down a bit as a few more heads popped out of the water. The students remaining in the pool quietly exited and fell in line with their peers.

"For the newbies, here is how today will work. I've already sorted everyone into groups based on your genetic structure and abilities. It is possible to change groups if need be, but for now, the groups will be as follows."

"Our three groups are Basans, YamYads and Kol Levs," Yara explained as she pointed to different points of the pool. "For example, if you're built like Shawn, who resembles the mighty blue whale, you are a Basan.

"The second group, YamYads, have a balance of strength and speed. Olive, Holly, Franklin, and Harper are all YamYads." Yara again pointed to the middle of the pool for those students to line up.

"Our final group is called Kol Levs. This includes Natalie, Ava, and Logabet. Kol Levs are fast and precise. They can fly through the water with ease and strike with absolute power." As Yara spoke she looked deep into Ava's eyes as if she was trying to send a hidden message. "The Kol Levs resemble some of the fastest fish in the sea. For example, Ava resembles the beautiful but deadly sailfish."

"Just soooo beautiful . . ." Natalie said to Ava in a sarcastic voice, prompting a quick laugh from one of Natalie's friends.

"And deadly," Ava added.

"Look at you with some spunk," Harper remarked towards Ava.

"Enough! Two at a time, you will race to the end of the pool and back. I want to get an idea of your technique and speed," Yara directed.

Ava looked down the line and saw Natalie smirking.

"Of course, she has to be in this class," Ava groaned.

Yara continued. "Shawn, Abigail, Hector, and Hannah, you will be racing first. Shawn versus Hector, then Abigail against Hannah."

Shawn and Hector got into ready position and stood at the edge of the pool, awaiting Yara's signal to start. The class was silent. Ava felt the tension in the room rise.

"*Yatza*!" Yara shouted.

The two boys dove into the pool. The surface barely rippled as they entered the water with hardly a splash. Ava's mind snapped into competition mode as she focused on Hector peeking over to assess the distance from his opponent. She wanted to laugh at the rookie move. Ava had always been taught never to do this, as it jeopardizes a swimmer's speed and is a huge distraction. She started to form her own plan of attack. She carried the confidence of being a swimming champion, but knew this race was going to be different. Not only was this a much larger and deeper pool, but Ava wasn't racing humans anymore. Yet, in that moment, Ava realized she wasn't human either; she, too, was an Acathodian. She took a deep breath. It was time to accept this strange new world—after all, she fit right in.

Before long, the boys' heads were out of the water and Shawn was celebrating his victory. Hector was noticeably upset, but when Shawn reached down to help him out of the pool, he took his hand to show that he harbored no hard feelings.

Though she could not sit in the locker room and carry out her usual pre-race mental routine, Ava tried to calm down and control her breathing as she waited for the others to finish their races. Just as she emerged from her meditation, the race between Hannah and Abigail had concluded.

"Olive and Holly, you're next. Please line up," Yara said, signaling the start of the YamYads race.

It was difficult for Ava to determine which students looked more like dolphins or sharks, but Ava could plainly see that Holly had shark-like qualities. Her head was slightly oblong, and her eyes stood far apart. She even had sharp, pointed teeth. Olive had smooth blue skin and a long beaky nose. The two students went to the edge of the pool and stood ready. They did not shake hands.

"*Yatza*!" Yara shouted to signal the start of the race.

Ava didn't pay much attention to the race. She had to clear her mind and stay focused on her own.

"Franklin and Harper, you're up," Yara instructed.

Ava was instantly taken out of her mental preparation; she couldn't help but give Harper her full attention. Harper seemed to have good focus, but she looked nervous. Ava was sure she felt more nervous for Harper than she had been for herself.

Harper and Franklin were set and waiting.

"*Yatza*!" Yara shouted.

Harper and Franklin dove into the water. Initially, Franklin took the lead, but it was clear that Harper was building up her speed. While Franklin kept a consistent but fast pace, Harper built momentum with every stroke, and shortly overtook her opponent. Harper was amazingly quick. Ava started to cheer as Harper neared the end of the pool. With an impressive final splash, Harper breached the water and touched the wall, winning the race. Harper waited for Franklin to exit the pool to give him a hug. They both walked back to their place in line with big smiles.

"Harper, you clocked in at one minute and fifty-three seconds. Franklin, you were close behind at one minute and fifty-eight seconds. Not bad at all," Yara said proudly.

Ava gave Harper a high five, but before Ava could stop smiling for Harper's big win Natalie's voice pierced Ava's ears and drowned her smile.

"I want to face Ava," Natalie demanded. She glared at Ava.

"Okay . . . Let's go for it," Yara said.

Yara shrugged at the aggressive demand from Natalie. Maybe she even wanted to see this race for herself.

Ava felt the blood drain from her face. This race would not change how Natalie felt about her; she was damned no matter the outcome. If Ava lost, Natalie would rub this in her face for eternity. But if she won, Natalie would probably be even more of a bully, and update her dictionary of insults.

"You got this Ava, just relax," Harper encouraged, as Ava took her position at the edge of the pool.

Ava looked around the class and saw all the other students looking at her with hopeful smiles. It was the same look that the students and teachers at her old school had given her before her swimming championship. The familiar pressure to win washed over Ava's soul, had her heart beating fast and hard.

"Now I know why everybody talks about you behind your back," Natalie mumbled so only Ava could hear.

"That's interesting, seeing as I just got here last night," Ava shot back.

"Well, that's when that awful smell arrived, too."

Ava did her best to ignore her. Natalie was only trying to get in her head.

"Okay, okay, ladies. Get in ready position,"

Ava's breath was not set. She tried to calm down and focus, but her thoughts on how much she despised Natalie were front and center.

The room fell silent.

"*Yatza*!"

Ava didn't miss a beat, but Natalie was just as fierce. Both girls flew into the pool at lightning speed. Ava powered forward, the water gliding seamlessly past her body, but her stroke was off. She was too in her head and having difficulty connecting with the water around her. Natalie was soon in the lead. As Ava pushed harder, memories of Kevin and her mother creeped into her mind, filling her heart with an overwhelming and overpowering sadness.

Just when she didn't think she could bear any more emotion, Ava felt a warmth radiating from her chest. At first, she thought the bottom of the pool was glowing, but then she saw the cord and the pendant, and realized it was emitting a soft, silvery light.

At that moment, Ava heard her mother's voice in her head. *I love you, Ava. I'm always with you.*

The voice was clear as a bell, as if her mother were right beside her. Ava felt a burst of energy and regained her focus.

Her mother's voice kept cheering her on. *Swim faster, Ava! You can do this!*

She sensed Natalie by her side as she picked up even more speed. The end of the pool was approaching quickly. With all her might, Ava pushed herself one last time and her fingers touched the wall. Both girls pulled their heads out of the water and looked around to see who had won. Natalie looked just as perplexed as Ava.

"Well?" Natalie asked Yara.

"That was amazing ladies," Yara said. "The winner was . . . Natalie."

"*Yes*!" Natalie screamed, pumping her fist in the air. "See! I knew I could beat you!"

Natalie jumped out of the pool and proudly strutted back to her classmates at the far wall of the Pool Hall.

Ava shook her head and dragged herself out of the water. She had never lost a race, but she didn't want to be a sore loser. Screwing up her mouth into a tight smile, Ava quickly walked over to Natalie with her hand out to offer congratulations.

"Ha! I'm not shaking that nasty hand," Natalie said abruptly, batting Ava's hand away. "Loser!"

Before she had time to register this new insult, Harper came bounding over and whisked her away to the other end of the line.

"Ava, you were so fast! I mean, I hate Natalie, but you were both incredible. I had no idea you could swim like that!"

"Yeah . . . I probably could have won if I had started off better," Ava said.

"Definitely! This is only your first day, so there's a lot more to learn. And if this is how fast you are now, I can't even dream of what you'll be able to do by the end of the semester," Harper said, giving her a pat on the back.

Ava smiled. Thank goodness for Harper. Without her, she wasn't sure where she'd be.

"Natalie had the best run today, swimming the length of the pool in one minute and thirty-two seconds. Ava, you were incredibly close behind at one minute and thirty-two point two seconds. Those are incredible times, ladies, but don't be fooled—you still have a long way to go. The school's record for the Kol Levs group is twenty-three seconds."

The entire class laughed almost in disbelief. All except Natalie and Ava. Instead, they exchanged a quick glance, as if to see whether the other would be up to the challenge.

"All right, that's it for today," Yara said, breaking the tension. "Go get changed, and I will see you all tomorrow. Ava, please come see me before you leave."

Ava quickly put on a fresh set of clothes and went to find Yara.

"What an amazing class today," she gushed to her new teacher.

"Thank you. You are truly a wonderful swimmer. I wanted to ask about your necklace, if you feel comfortable talking about it. Is it from your mom?"

Ava looked down at the blue pendant. "Yes, she gave it to me shortly before I left home to come here."

"I see. This is a very special gift. Did she tell you its history?" Yara asked.

"No, not really. But something very strange happened while I was racing. I could hear her voice and felt this sudden rush of energy."

Yara nodded. "There is a strong power to this necklace. It is very old and rare. Next time you see your mom, you should ask her about it. And remember to always keep it on—you don't want something that powerful falling into the wrong hands."

"Will do," Ava said, placing a hand protectively over her chest. "Thank you, Yara."

As Ava walked away the words "the wrong hands" echoed in her thoughts. Whose hands were those?

11

Live and Learn

"What's with the face?" Harper said as they left the Pool Hall. "You almost won today."

"Yeah, but I lost by two tenths of a second—"

"Ava, that's practically nothing," Harper interrupted. "Don't obsess over it."

"You're right, Harper, it shouldn't matter. Just must be off my game a bit."

When the girls reached the dining hall, they dropped their bags on the same wooden table they had eaten at earlier. Harper pursed her lips and let out a sharp breath. "Well, my mother once said, 'you never truly lose if you learn from your loss.' I like to think she's right. It makes the world a lot easier to live in."

Ava played those words over in her head. They made sense. She *had* learned something—that no matter how good she was, there would always be someone faster. "Wow, wise words from your mom. What's your mother like?"

"She's an amazing woman. Strong. She had to deal with a lot . . . We both did." Ava stayed silent, waiting for Harper to continue. They loaded their trays with food and returned to their seats. "My dad was in the army overseas. About a year ago, he was killed in action, leaving me and my mom alone."

She glanced at Ava before quickly shifting her gaze to her plate.

"Most people get sort of awkward when I say that. They don't know how to deal with a kid who just lost her father," Harper said as tears welled up in her eyes.

Ava reached across the table to hold Harper's hand. "No wonder we get along."

"Huh?"

"I once thought my father died in a car accident. I've since learned that he in fact was killed in some Acathodian battle. My mom raised me on her own."

Harper's eyes lit up. "Maybe we should start a Raised-By-Widowed-Mothers Club."

"That would be *totally* depressing," Ava said; to which Harper nodded. Before things could get too sad, Ava changed the subject. "On a good note, you won your race."

Harper reached for her water glass and raised it high. "And you killed your first attack dummy!"

"You bet I did!" Ava clinked her glass against her friend's.

"And . . . I know you have a boyfriend back home, but Joshua seems to like you," Harper added. "Are you excited to see him tomorrow?"

Ava thought of Kevin and shrugged. She loved him but had nearly convinced herself that she would never see him again. Even if she did, it would never be the same. Her heart twisted at the thought.

"I guess I'm a little excited, but I don't know how I'm supposed to feel," Ava said, trailing off. She cleared her throat. "I guess I wasn't completely honest earlier."

"Oh?" Harper raised an eyebrow.

Ava took a deep breath. "I broke up with Kevin right before I came here. I mean, what choice did I have, you know? But I still love him and miss him terribly, and I don't know how to stop thinking about him."

"Aw, he sounds really special." Harper gave Ava's hand a tight squeeze. "Breakups are the worst, but you gotta give yourself time. You only split up two days ago, take your time. It's going to take a minute for you to feel alright again."

"I know," Ava murmured. "I'm just really impatient and I wish the pain would go away."

"Hey. You got this. You're already kicking butt at your new school. And no harm in having Joshua as a friend . . . for now," Harper said with a wink.

"Thanks, Harp. But really, who needs boys when I've got great friends like you?"

Harper laughed. "I'm sure you'll change your mind about that someday, but for now I'll take it."

"We'll see," Ava said, absentmindedly. She noticed that the light filtering through the stained-glass windows was growing dim, signaling that bedtime was approaching.

"Well, I am beat," Harper said with a big yawn. "I'm going to head to bed."

The girls put away their plates and parted ways with a hug and a promise to find each other tomorrow. Ava finally reached her room and tried to push open her door, but it did not budge.

What the heck is going on? She pushed harder, but still, the door wouldn't move.

Finally, it hit her. She wanted to kick herself for not remembering sooner.

"Esh-my-eem."

The door opened gently, and a calming breeze blew past her. As Ava walked into her room, the door shut behind her. Slowly pacing around her room to process the day's events, she looked at the old furniture, the various tapestries on the wall of placid, underwater scenes. Everything in the room seemed to echo some distant past. Alone, now, for the first time since she'd arrived at the school, the silence was deafening, and an empty longing hit her, full force. It was easy to mask these feelings when distracted, but once the lights went out, there was nothing holding back the chains of her emotions and fears.

Ava's eyes turned toward her desk. A feathered quill pen loomed over a tiny jar of ink, both perched atop her antique wooden desk. Looking in the drawers, Ava discovered a few books with the same blue tinted paper that she had seen other students use for notetaking. Then, she noticed a brown leather backpack resting near her bed. She opened the bag to reveal an arsenal of textbooks, notebooks, paper, and pens.

Ava smiled sleepily. *Ezra must have dropped these off for me.*

Knowing she had Ezra looking out for her shaved off the loneliness and replaced it with enough confidence to face whatever challenges tomorrow might offer. Ava yawned, flopped on her bed, and fell asleep.

Ava woke to the sound of birds singing and waves crashing, seemingly right outside her door. She had no idea what time it was but thought it couldn't be later than seven in the morning. Before she could fully open her eyes, a loud knock made her jump.

"Ava, are you awake?"

Still cocooned in her blankets, Ava croaked her password and the door opened, revealing Harper with a leather-bound book in hand. Harper rushed into the room and jumped on Ava's bed.

"Whoa, that was so cool! I didn't know some rooms had passwords."

"Mhm . . ." Ava started sleepily, but then a thought occurred to her, jolting her awake. "I thought all the rooms had passwords."

"No. Yours is the first I've seen."

Weird, she thought, wiping the sleep from her eyes. Why was her room different? Just another question to ask Ezra later.

"I was doing some research in the library this morning and . . ." Harper flipped the book open to a place she had been holding with her index finger. "Look what I found."

Ava shook herself awake and looked down at the page. There was a picture of the very necklace her mother had given her. Gasping, she blinked the caption into focus and read aloud:

"This necklace was crafted and worn by the Lady of the Lake. It is said that the necklace has the power to enhance the gifts of any being that possesses it. Little is known about the necklace or its whereabouts, but it was last seen in the possession of a cave-dweller in the underwater metropolis of Hadal. Though much myth surrounds this artifact, it undoubtedly holds great power."

Great power. The words echoed in her mind as she stroked the pendant. At first cold, it instantly warmed to her touch.

"How did you find this?" Ava asked.

"Well, lucky for you, I had a feeling I had already seen that necklace somewhere before. I don't really sleep much, so I went looking for it."

"This is amazing!" Ava said. "But it can't be the same. Mine is probably just a replica."

Harper's nose wrinkled. "Why would you say that?"

"Because, for one, I *don't* have great power. I lost to Natalie yesterday."

"Maybe it is. But it looks real. Don't you want to know if you are wearing a necklace made by the *Lady of the Lake?*" Harper said, bursting with excitement.

"I think I would be more excited if I knew who the Lady of the Lake was," Ava admitted.

"Ava, the Lady of the Lake is one of the most powerful sorceresses in the world. She has forged some of the most incredible magical items known to us. Like King Arthur's sword, Excalibur," Harper said, her voice low and serious, so serious, Ava thought she had to be pulling her leg.

When her expression didn't change, Ava said, "Oh, that's a real thing?"

"Yes, and so is she. Though some say that anyone who approaches her is either killed or goes missing," Harper said. "But that's only if you can find her."

Ava touched a finger to her necklace again. "Okay, so . . . how would I know if it's real?"

"I guess we see what this thing can do."

"I like the sound of that. I'll ask Ezra when I see him—he seems like he would know something about it. Yara sounded like she knew something as well."

"Ezra always starts his day in the dining hall, so we can probably talk to him there. Also, I'm starving so . . . let's go."

Harper hopped off Ava's bed, landing on her feet without a sound.

"Let me get dressed and I'll meet you down there."

"Sounds like a plan. I'll leave the book with you, but don't forget to return it. I don't want to be paying any late fees."

As soon as Harper left, Ava looked at the book again. There wasn't any more information regarding the necklace, but despite what she'd said to Harper, there was no doubt in Ava's mind that this was the object she had around her neck. Ava had already felt the power coursing through her when she swam. Though she had wanted to believe that it was her new Acathodian abilities shining through, she suspected that the necklace was partly responsible. She couldn't wait to find out what else this relic could do.

By the time Ava got down to the dining hall, Harper was already eating her breakfast. Ava loaded her tray with white fish salad and a variety of fresh fruits. Once she had no more room on her plate, she joined Harper at the table.

“So, here’s the deal,” Harper said with the intensity of a CIA agent. “Ezra usually comes down in the morning to eat and to socialize with students. It’s good for his image. That’s a good time for us to ask him about the necklace.”

“Sounds good. He was my mother’s best friend when they were growing up, so that will give us an easy in.”

Ava started to lose focus as she shoveled fish into her mouth faster and faster. She couldn’t get enough of the food in front of her.

“This is so good,” Ava said through a mouthful of melon.

Harper laughed. “Slow it down Ava, there’s plenty more to go around. Also, I don’t want to have to give you the Heimlich.”

Ava looked up; mouth still full of food. She swallowed before speaking. “So, when does this uncontrollable hunger stop?”

“Eventually you’ll get used to it and your eating will slow down.”

“I hope so,” Ava said, stuffing her mouth again.

“I mean, look at me,” Harper said confidently. “One bite at a time, and then I breathe.”

Harper demonstrated with an exaggerated inhale. From the corner of her eye, Ava saw a blue and yellow figure enter the dining hall. “There he is.”

Harper stood up quickly. “Let’s go! Before someone else gets to him!”

The girls quickly walked over to Ezra and Harper tapped his shoulder lightly. “Hey, Ezra!”

“Good morning, ladies,” Ezra said with a pleasant nod.

“Ezra, do you know anything about this necklace that my mother gave me?” Ava blurted. Looking around, embarrassed, she lowered her voice. “Is it the one made by the Lady of the Lake.”

Ezra cocked his head to look at the blue pendant. “I don’t know much. Your mother got the necklace sometime before she left Hadal, but unfortunately the only people who know exactly how she did that are your mom and the Lady herself.”

Noticing the disappointment on Ava’s face, Ezra held up a finger.

"Tell you what. I'll call your mom tomorrow and she can come visit in a few weeks. I need to speak with her as well."

"Sounds wonderful!" Ava said.

Ezra quickly walked away to stop a student from throwing food at another student.

"I wish my cell worked out here," Ava said.

"Yeah, no phone does, except Ezra's office phone. You can ask him to use it when you want," Harper said with her mouth full.

"Yeah, I guess one phone is better than no phone," Ava sighed.

Harper looked past Ava's shoulder at the clock. "Crap! It's almost nine! History class is starting in five minutes."

"Ah! Already?"

The girls grabbed their bags and took off running out of the dining hall.

When they entered class, out of breath and still giggling, Professor Lundlow was already writing something on the board.

"Today, we are going to answer the most important question of the year: Who are we?" He paused for dramatic effect.

"In this lecture, we will discuss the history of the Acathodians and the impact we have had on our surroundings. As you were once students of the human world, you've learned that some sea-based creatures have developed the ability to breathe on land. Those same creatures not only began to breathe oxygen, but their fins also morphed into hands with fingers and feet with toes. Their scales smoothed over and became porous so that hair could grow and help them adapt to the ever-changing weather. As it turns out, those little critters were not little at all—they were the Acathodians. We were the very first beings that roamed the earth. Over thousands of years, we evolved into what you now know as 'humans.' We are the spark of life, the common ancestor that links all present-day Acathodians, humans, and mermaids."

A student slowly raised his hand.

"Yes, Mr. Ruby?"

"If we evolved from Acathodians to become humans, why are we turning back into Acathodians?"

"Great question!" Professor Lundlow rocked back on his heels, leaning against his desk, which wobbled against his weight. "Our genetic code is full of Acathodian DNA. In fact, every living creature in sea or on land is derived from Acathodians. We are the common ancestor to all life. In many cases, something activated that portion of the code to kickstart the transformation from human back to Acathodian. Though we understand how this happens, we are still unsure of what triggers the response. It could be stress, the changing environment, external threats, or a host of other possibilities. We also don't know why so few transform while others remain human. Interesting, right?"

Lundlow jumped off his desk and started to walk around the room.

"For instance: Mr. Ruby, you have dark, smooth scales and red eyes. Ms. Sachar, your skin is yellow and orange, but your eyes are big and blue. Just wait until you get into the deepest part of the ocean—those eyes will allow you to see clear as day!"

The girl reached up to adjust her glasses and smiled softly.

The professor continued. "Mr. Franklin, your skin has spikes that will get sharper and larger with time. Ms. Greene, your hair wonderfully matches the colors and consistency of seaweed and will permit you to blend in when danger arises."

Ava touched her hair self-consciously.

"All the qualities you have are unique to your family's bloodline. Not just how you look, but also the special abilities you may gain over time. These are links to our Acathodian history, as well as to your individual past. This is who we are. Be proud of your lineage: it will always serve an important purpose."

Lundlow continued with his lecture. Ava became so entranced by his lesson, she was caught off guard by the ringing of the gong.

Ava and Harper got up from their seats, making a beeline for their self-defense class. The girls entered the practice arena to find Agatha already whipping the class into shape. They ran to their preferred weapon walls, where Ava found the same knives she had used last time. Today, however, another knife drew her attention. The weapon was curved and about a foot long. She had a good feeling about it. She picked up the knife and tossed it into the air a few times. It was heavy, but manageable.

Looking around at the rest of the students sparring in the room, Ava was a bit lost. After she had picked up her weapon, she wasn't sure what to do next. She walked over to Agatha, who was helping her latest opponent up from the mat.

"Excuse me, Agatha?" Ava said hesitantly.

"Speak up, Ava, be confident."

"What should I be doing?" Ava asked, trying hard to sound more at ease.

"Good, you showed some initiative. Unlike Jerzey over there . . . Jerzey! Get over here, now!" Agatha screamed.

Jerzey was a large boy who looked more like a deformed dolphin than a human. He had a flat nose and small beady brown eyes bulged out of his head.

"Ava, meet Jerzey. Jerzey is new as well. You will be sparring partners for this year." Agatha looked at Ava and chuckled when she saw the razor-sharp foot-long blade. "You can grab the wooden sparring weapons at the table in the back of the room."

Slightly disappointed that she wouldn't be trained in using it, Ava hung her knife back on the wall. At least she would be fighting with a living partner this time.

"Practice self-defense," Agatha directed. "Each of you has five chances to land a hit while the other defends. Then, switch roles. First one with a hundred clean hits wins."

Ava and Jerzey looked at one another blankly for a moment.

"Well, off you go!" Agatha prompted.

The two headed back to the sparring section—which was unfortunately not such an easy task, as they had to dodge stray sword swipes from their classmates. Ava narrowly missed getting hit in the face by a club. When they arrived at the table, slightly shaken by the ordeal, Ava saw wooden daggers that she thought would be a good substitute for her curved knife. She grabbed two of them, one for each hand. Jerzey chose a long spear.

"Okay, ready?" Jerzey said, as they got settled in the back corner of the room.

"Let's do it. You can attack first," Ava offered.

Jerzey swung the spear at Ava's chest, but Ava quickly dodged it. Clumsily, he waved his weapon once again, this time screaming the word "two." He seemed to be counting his attempted strikes. Ava tried not to smile as she realized that he was stopping and resetting after every strike.

"Three!" Jerzey said with more enthusiasm, this time aiming for Ava's head.

Ava ducked with plenty of time, realizing that she was much faster than her opponent.

When it was her turn, Ava decided to pursue a different strategy. First, she knocked Jerzey's spear to one side; an enormous clang echoed through the arena. Before he had time to realize what she was doing, she rushed inward to his body, landing a solid strike to his stomach. Jerzey turned and swung his spear around, desperately trying to hit his assailant. But Ava was already on the move, and she landed another clean hit to Jerzey's back, sending him sprawling to the floor. Though her opponent was clearly defeated, Ava didn't let up. She kicked the spear out of Jerzey's hands and then crouched down, so she was almost sitting on his stomach.

"Four and five," Ava said as she playfully tapped the knife to Jerzey's chest.

"Wow, that was amazing," Jerzey said. "I thought you were new to this! What was that? Kung Fu or something?"

Ava laughed and helped Jerzey to his feet. "Krav Maga, two years. I guess I just picked it up better than I thought."

"Well, that was unbelievable. I think I can definitely learn a lot from you."

Ava got into a fighting stance. "Okay, enough chit chat. Now, try to hit me . . . if you can, that is."

Ava was smart to be on her guard. Jerzey was a quick learner, and he was moving much faster now. She spun and dove out of the way, just missing the tip of Jerzey's spear on a few occasions. They went back and forth for a while, falling into a rhythm of strikes and parries. As Ava dodged another attack, her eyes fell on Josh, who was just walking into the room. Distracted, she didn't see the hard thrust of Jerzey's spear that landed squarely between her ribs. Ava went down hard.

Jerzey dropped his spear and rushed toward her. "Ava, are you okay? I am so sorry!"

Ava grabbed her side as she curled up on the floor in agony.

"Agatha!" Jerzey screamed.

Agatha came running over and bent down next to Ava. "You're going to be fine, Ava. Drink this."

Agatha handed her an odd smelling brew. As she gulped it down, a sharp pain radiated from her abdomen. Ava let out a shriek—she could hear the sound of her rib cracking back into place. The pain was gone as quickly as it had started, and Ava began to feel as good as new. She held a hand to her side in amazement, then searched around for the reason she'd lost focus.

But she couldn't see Joshua anywhere.

Agatha gave Jerzey a thumbs-up. "Nice hit!"

Jerzey shook his head in disbelief. "She was kicking my butt the entire period! She hit me like, eighty-four times!"

"Well, how many times did you get a clean hit in?" Agatha asked.

"Once! Literally just that one." Jerzey pointed to Ava, who was still on the ground catching her breath.

"What happened?"

"I learned a lesson," Ava said, still breathing hard as she scanned the arena for Josh.

"And what lesson was that?" Agatha asked.

"Don't lose focus."

"That's my girl!" Agatha said, helping Ava to her feet. "Okay, you two can end a bit early today."

"No way!" Ava exclaimed. "I still need sixteen hits!"

Jerzey groaned.

"Alright then, back to your places," Agatha said with a shrug, heading back to the sidelines.

Ava unleashed her sword from its sheath and raised it high. The other students rushed over to observe, and this time, Ava willed her focus not to stray from her opponent. Agatha waved her sword down.

"Rok Kazock!" she screamed, rushing full force into the attack.

12

Safe Haven

Sixteen hits later, Ava looked around the training room, exhilarated. She couldn't help but laugh at the fact that she had just won her first combat battle. She had gone from playing dodgeball to dodging deadly weapons, and she loved it. This new life, this new reality, was what Ava had been missing all along.

"Ava!" an excited voice called.

She turned to see Joshua running toward her. So, he *had* been there.

"That was outstanding!"

"Thank you! But clearly, I still have a lot to learn."

"Yes, but for one of your first fights you were amazing! Soon you'll probably be able to beat me," Joshua said with a chuckle. "I know we said five, but would you want a tour of the school now?"

Ava's heart leapt with excitement and plummeted to her stomach, all in the space of a couple of seconds. "I can't . . . I have swimming class with Yara now."

"No, you don't!" Harper called, running up to the two of them.

She was out of breath and had blood trickling down the side of her face.

"Uh, Harper? You're bleeding," Ava said, pointing out the obvious.

"Oh, yeah." Harper brushed a strand of blue hair out of the way with a shrug. "Mr. Blob got me with a good left hook. It is what it is."

Ava looked over and saw a boy that looked a bit like an amoeba with legs. "I was going to say, 'be nice,' but dang, he really does look like a blob."

Harper and Joshua laughed.

"Ava, Mr. Blob's DNA is linked to a blobfish," Harper explained. "It's not an insult, he really is a blob."

"Ah I see," Ava said, still slightly amused. "But anyway, you said we don't have class?"

"Yeah. Usually we would now, but Yara canceled it. I just heard from someone who said she saw a sign on the door."

"Perfect," Joshua said. He put his hand out, directing Ava toward the door. "Shall we?"

"I will take that as my cue to exit. Alright Mr. Blob, round nine, ding ding!" Harper shouted as she ran back to her fighting partner.

Ava looked at Josh. "I guess we shall."

As she and Joshua went through the main doors, Ava realized this was the first time in two days that she had been outside the school walls. She saw students kicking a ball around and playing catch on the white sandy beach. The beautiful turquoise waves calmly resolved onto the shore and the sun's rays made the water sparkle.

"Are we going to the beach?" Ava asked.

"Not today," Joshua replied coolly. "The beach is beautiful, but it's no place for plebes."

"Plebes?"

"Newcomers," he clarified.

Ava folded her arms. "The waves don't look that rough."

"It's not the waves . . . it's what lurks beneath. Acathodians have many enemies and sometimes they like to hang around this area, waiting to strike. Unlike the human world, they know we're here."

A wave of dread washed over her.

"Don't worry, Ava," Joshua said, reading her thoughts. "By the time you're ready to go into the sea, nothing will scare you. Come this way."

He led Ava away from the water and toward a group of petrified trees with brilliant green leaves. The trees rose high above the school, but some light still managed to sneak past the foliage. The sun reflected off the petrified trunks, creating an astonishing array of brilliant colors that made the forest gleam. Joshua and Ava traveled deeper into the woods. The white sand started to fade as mossy pebbles, rocks, and stones took its place. As they moved farther from the school, Ava felt alive in a way she never had before. She took a few deep breaths to smell the piney air.

Joshua came to a sudden stop. "Close your eyes, Ava."

She obliged with hesitation.

"Do you hear it?" he asked.

"I hear . . . water?" Ava opened her eyes.

"That means we're almost there!"

Joshua offered Ava his hand to help her over a fallen log. She took it, surprised at how comfortable it felt. Different from Kevin's, but comfortable. Safe. The sound of rushing water grew louder as they traveled down the hill. After turning on to a lightly traveled path, they came across an exquisite, burbling stream. A faint mist embraced the water as if the two elements were dancing together to the song of nature.

Joshua and Ava silently took in the view. A few feet away, Ava noticed a wooden bench that had been constructed from fallen logs.

"I made it myself," Joshua stated proudly.

"What, the stream?" Ava teased.

"Very funny," Joshua said.

"It looks like a very nice and sturdy bench!" she said, testing it out. "How did you find this place?"

He sat down next to her. "During my first year here, I was going through a tough time. Ezra saw that I needed someplace to escape and just pointed the way. I cleared the path, built the bench and this has been my safe haven ever since."

"I guess we all need a safe haven sometimes," Ava said. "I can see why you chose this place; it's so peaceful."

"I come here whenever I need to meditate, or just to think," Josh said.

It was his safe place, his refuge, and he'd taken her here. She couldn't help but be touched by the gesture, sharing such an intimate part of himself. Unless he brought all his girls here?

Probably. He was the most popular guy on campus, after all. Her mind stirred with questions. She wanted to peel back his layers.

She didn't want to pry, but she found herself asking, "What were you going through that made you need an escape?"

Josh paused. "Well, leaving home wasn't the tough part. Let's just say my father wasn't the best man in the world and he only got worse when my mother passed away.

"I am so sorry, Josh. That couldn't have been easy."

"I mean, I was happy to get here and be away from my father. The Land School has been a blessing," Joshua smiled.

"You don't miss your old school?" Ava asked.

He shrugged. "Enough about me. How are you doing?"

"To be honest, confused. I'm kind of homesick yet, feel at home."

Joshua gestured at the stream and the trees around them. "Well, mi casa es su casa."

"Thanks, that means a lot," Ava said. "So, let me guess, you bring all the girls here?"

Joshua looked at Ava a bit sheepishly. "Actually, you are the first."

Just then, a deep horn sounded through the air. He stiffened. "Ava, we have to go."

"What's going on?"

"We need to get back to the school, now," he repeated, glancing around anxiously.

They jumped up and started to run back to school. They wove through the trees and jumped over rocks and branches. Once a beautiful woodland, the forest had become a dangerous obstacle course. Ava had no time to appreciate any of the beauty as she followed Joshua past every tree. He was a muscular guy, but he moved with great agility. She didn't know what the sound meant, but suspected danger was near.

"Stay close to me, Ava," Joshua called over his shoulder, moving at a breakneck clip.

When they reached the school, they slowed their pace and hugged the sidewall as they neared the front entrance.

That's when she saw it, and her blood ran cold.

13

WHAT DID I GET MYSELF INTO?

The growling, grotesque grindylow was tall and had scaly skin the color of wet seaweed. The creature's red eyes locked onto Ava as it bounded toward the terrified teenagers, blade-like jaws glistening with saliva.

Just then the front door of the school shot open.

"Inside! Both of you!" a strong voice called out.

Ezra grabbed Joshua and Ava by the arms and ushered them into the building. Ava saw a bunch of students crowding around to look out the windows.

As the door closed behind him, Ezra walked fearlessly toward the beached grindylow. He stood tall in dark, metallic armor and held a long golden-bladed sword. The grindylow wailed, baring its razor-sharp teeth and nails. It showed no fear as it started to race towards Ezra, closing the distance at a rapid speed. When they were mere feet apart, they both leapt forward to attack. Ezra dodged a lethal claw and sliced upward through the grindylow's stomach. The creature fell to the ground in two clean halves.

"Well, that was anticlimactic," Ava heard one student say. Bloody sword still raised, Ezra circled the area, checking for additional threats, then calmly made his way back toward the school.

"Okay, everyone," Yara said, clapping sharply to get the students' attention. "Back to class, or whatever you were doing."

Ezra opened the door, looking as cheerful as if he were about to greet a new student. He seemed so relaxed.

"What is everybody standing around for?" Ezra asked.

The students all laughed and broke into applause. Ezra played along and took a sweeping bow.

Her long braid swaying by her hips, Yara walked over and placed a hand on Ezra's shoulder.

"I still got it, huh?" Ezra asked her.

"You never lost it," she replied.

"Good thing it was only one of them, or this would have been a very bad situation," Ezra admitted.

"Well, one can be hard enough to take down." Yara moved her hand on Ezra's back. "You did it as easily as slicing a melon."

"Are the two of them like . . . a thing?" Ava asked, surprisingly more interested in the gossip than Ezra killing a monster.

"No one knows, but we all think so. The more concerning matter is the grindylow." Joshua replied. "They're pretty rare. Especially this close to the school."

"Man, that made me hungry!" Harper had somehow materialized behind Joshua and Ava.

"Harper, you didn't even fight! You just watched," Joshua chided.

"Yeah . . . But I watched *intensely*!"

The three laughed, and all the tension faded away.

"I'm getting hungry, too," Joshua said. "Let's go eat."

"I'll be right there," Ava said. "I need to talk to Yara."

She approached Yara, who was still chatting with Ezra. "Sorry to butt in, but, Yara, do you have a minute?"

Ezra took the opportunity to excuse himself, and Yara turned to her student.

"Yara, back when you first saw my necklace, I got the sense that you knew something about it." Ava looked down and held her necklace. "I just learned that it was made by the Lady of the Lake."

She blinked. "Yes. It is."

"I understand that she's very powerful?" Ava confirmed.

"Her power is unmatched. No one dares to cross her, and no one dares to face her. Well . . . no one dared, until your mother."

"Why did my mom face her?" Ava asked.

"I don't know. I was friends with her and your father, but not as close as Ezra was. Those three were always getting into trouble together, but I don't think even Ezra knows the full story."

"Yeah, I asked, and he didn't know much either." Ava's spirits dropped. "Okay. Well thanks."

Yara sighed. "Sorry I don't have more information for you. Although, I will say that I once saw your mother fighting more enemies than I could count, and she just got more ruthless with every approaching foe. She was so fast and cunning; it was truly a sight to behold. Her blade passed through the enemy as easily as if it were air. If not the power of the necklace, I don't know how she did those things."

"My mother did that?" Ava asked in surprise.

"Even though I can't tell you much about that necklace, I can tell you for sure that your mother is quite the warrior . It's no wonder that the Lady of the Lake let her live that night."

Ava was in shock, but managed to utter a quiet "thank you."

"No problem, always happy to help. See you tomorrow," Yara said.

Ava took off toward the dining hall to share what she had learned with Harper. As she rounded the corner, she collided with Natalie.

"Watch where you're going, spaz," Natalie said, flinging her arms dramatically.

"Sorry, Natalie, I didn't see you there."

"Pfft . . . Your eyes are in the front of your head for a reason."

Ava took a deep breath and decided to take the high road. "Hey, Natalie . . . I know we've only been competitors so far, but it would be nice to have someone to talk to from back home. Maybe we can hang out sometime?"

Natalie approached so they were almost nose-to-nose. "Ava, just go away, okay? Like, forever and permanently?"

Then, she turned quickly, whipping her hair into Ava's face, and walked away. Ava calmed herself down and went to find Harper and Josh. They were sitting in the back of the dining hall with Mr. Blob and another girl she didn't recognize. Ava approached the table.

"Hi, I'm Ava," she said, introducing herself to Mr. Blob.

"Hey, I'm Jimmy, but friends call me Mr. Blob. I'm sure you've already figured that out though."

"Nice to meet you. I hear you have a nice left hook—you gave Harper a nice cut on her cheek," Ava said, nudging Harper.

Mr. Blob leaned past Ava, causing her to bend back out of the way. He locked eyes with Harper in mock intensity. "No one messes with Mr. Blob."

They all laughed.

"Oh, I'll get you next time," Harper said, throwing a piece of bread at him.

Mr. Blob laughed and shoved the bread into his mouth.

"Ava, I also want to introduce you to my friend Seal," Joshua said, gesturing to the dark eyed woman to his left.

Seal had a mysterious allure. Blue ink tattoos crawled up her wrists and her arms, and silver beads draped down from her neck. Concho earrings dangled from her lobes.

"Nice to meet you, Ava," Seal said, turning her attention back to the conversation. "That was crazy."

Ava sat down next to Harper as Mr. Blob said, "That was the fourth one this month."

"The sixth, actually," Seal corrected.

"There have been six? Why were we only warned about four of them?" Joshua asked. "We never used to see grindylows this close to campus. What the hell is going on?"

Seal shrugged. "Two of them turned away before Ezra or Agatha got to them."

"I would turn away, too, if Agatha was heading my way," Harper said. "Maybe the grindylows are smarter than we give them credit for."

"Never doubt the intelligence of an enemy, for that is a weakness that will surely lead to your demise," Seal said, quoting a phrase Ava had seen scrawled in various places around the school.

The rest of the group nodded in silent agreement.

"Seal, where are you from?" Ava asked.

"Arizona. I've lived in the Grand Canyon my entire life."

"Moving here from the desert must have been a big change," Ava remarked.

"Actually, it feels like turning into an Acathodian was my destiny. I live by the Havasu Falls, so water has always played a large role in my life. In my language, 'havasu' means 'blue-green water' and 'pai' means 'people,' so I wouldn't be surprised if most of my ancestors were Acathodians, too."

"Seal is without a doubt the coolest Acathodian of us all," Harper chimed in.

Seal smiled and stood up. "Sorry to leave so soon, but I need to rest after all this excitement."

"It was a pleasure to meet you, Ava," Mr. Blob said, following.

"Oh, the pleasure is all mine," she replied.

Ava, Harper, and Joshua continued to chat and joke around for a while longer, but soon the long day took its toll and Ava began to tire. She wished Harper and Joshua a good night and retreated to her room.

Ava awoke with a start. Time had flown so quickly at school she had almost forgotten that her mother was coming today. She couldn't wait to introduce her mom to her new friends—especially Joshua and Harper. With a spring in her step, Ava journeyed downstairs. When she didn't see her mother in the lobby waiting for her, she went into the dining hall for an early breakfast. The hallways were still quiet, as most of the other students were still asleep. Just as Ava was about to enter the dining hall, she overheard Ezra speaking.

"Things are getting worse here. We've had many more infiltrations this year than in any of the past fifteen. This month there were no less than thirty-five! We've kept it under the radar, but there were six grindylows that I am sure the students saw—I slayed another just yesterday. The tide is turning, and we need to be ready."

Ava gasped, flattening herself against the wall so she could listen without being seen. She had no idea the grindylows posed such a serious threat.

"We must send a message to Maridius," said a voice that Ava recognized as Yara's.

"Yet, that will be hard to do as communication with Hadal has been cut," Ezra responded.

"I agree." This was Agatha's voice. "We need to be extra strict with the students to make sure they can defend themselves."

"Sura, what do you think?" Ezra asked.

Ava shivered at the mention of her mother's name. Her mother was already here. But why was she in this meeting?

"I've seen these warning signs before. There will undoubtedly be an attack soon. The size of that attack and the readiness of the students remain to be seen. You must get them ready to fight. I fear that Isabella's army will soon be on its way."

Ava squeezed her eyes closed, trying without success to wrap her head around what was going on. The excitement over seeing her mother seemed to fade under these new concerns. Why were there so many secrets?

She and the other students deserved to know what was going on.

Bracing herself with a deep breath, she pulled herself from her hiding space and stepped into the dining hall to confront them.

But no one was there. She looked around in confusion. She was certain they were right around the corner.

"Ava is awake, please excuse me," she heard her mother state, then the scraping of chairs upon the floor.

Ava remained frozen in the center of the dining hall, still searching out her mother's voice, as her mother entered from the main entrance, a placid look on her face.

Relieved, Ava took a step toward her, but froze. "Mom, what the heck is going on? I heard everything! Also, how did I hear everything?"

"Everything is okay," Sura said calmly. "Let's go for a walk and I will explain."

Her mother put an arm around her and guided her out of the side door of the school, and the pair took a winding path down to the foot of the ocean. After hearing about those grindylows, Ava was hesitant to get too close to the lapping waves.

"Mom, we shouldn't go near the water. It's not safe."

"Nothing will harm us."

Ava attempted to match her mother's confidence as the two strode down to the sea. As they approached the water's edge, it flowed just up to their ankles. Ava was terrified of water for the first time in her life.

"Do not be scared, my love. This is who you are. Nothing will harm you."

Ava looked into her mother's deep green eyes. Until recently, Ava had believed that those same eyes had never told her a single lie. Now, she wasn't sure what to believe, or how to feel. Ava waded toward her mother, who was already waist deep in the water. She dug deep to find her confidence, taking one step after another. With each step, she worried that someone or something would grab her foot and pull her to the bottom of the ocean.

"I can do this," Ava whispered to herself. She really didn't have a choice.

"It's time to dive in, Ava. Swim!" Sura commanded.

Ava took a deep breath and submerged herself. All the fear left Ava's mind. A brilliant jolt of excitement overwhelmed Ava's body, followed by deep contentment, as if this was where she was meant to be. She was unable to control her emotions as she started gliding through the tides and slicing through the waves. Her skin gleamed, her hair thickened, and webbing appeared between her fingers and toes. The ocean gleamed with hues her eyes had never seen before. Ava swam freely, as if she was dancing and gliding through a maze of dappled lights.

Yet, this feeling did not last. A sudden sensation of heaviness paralyzed her. Elation quickly turned into despair. Her necklace started to weigh her down. Ava grabbed and clawed at it, desperately trying to unclasp it from her neck. But the necklace grew tighter and heavier. Ava's hands moved to her throat as if she was trying to break the grasp of an attacker's strangling grip. Her eyes stung, her arms now floating upward lifelessly. Ava's mind lingered on the last feeling she might ever have—her lungs burning from hopelessly holding her now stale breath. Darkness overcame Ava, and she fell deeper into the abyss.

It was then, when all the pain and fear faded that Ava opened her eyes and took her first breath.

Ava was reborn.

14

The Lady and the Necklace

Ava stood frozen in the golden sand. The ripple of the waves passed over her ankles. She listened to drops of water hitting the ocean's surface as they rolled off her skin. An unfamiliar power coursed through Ava's body, causing her to breathe heavily from the rush of adrenaline.

Not far away, Sura stood on the beach with a beaming smile. "How do you feel?"

"The necklace . . ." Ava started to say with a tinge of anger and fright.

"Did exactly what it had to do," Sura finished.

Ava stayed silent. She could feel her heart beating, a reminder she was alive. It would have been easy to focus on the sharp pain and fear, but with such power coursing through her body now, that was all but forgotten.

"How do you feel?" Sura repeated.

"Different. But . . . not a bad different. Good." Her head snapped to her mother's as she asked the question that had been marinating in her head since the moment the transformation happened. "Mom. Did I just breathe underwater?"

"It's an incredible feeling, isn't it? Let's get you dried off and head back inside."

I did. I breathed underwater. Like a fish. Like . . . who I truly am. An Acathodian.

Once Ava and Sura returned to the school, Ava noticed something different. Every student they passed was staring at her. When she got to the mirror in her room, she realized why. The figure looking back was a fully evolved Acathodian.

Ava had never felt so beautiful. The orange and purple patterns on her skin were more vibrant than ever before, and her thick hair now had more prominent hints of blue mixed in with the purple. Her large, round eyes reflected magnificent shades of yellow, blue, and orange. Ava looked down at her hands and feet. Her skin was different, but it surprised her to see that there was no webbing between her fingers and toes. She didn't feel like a schoolgirl anymore—she was a strong and beautiful woman. After staring at her new self for a few minutes, Ava left her bathroom and jumped onto the bed next to Sura.

"Okay, first question: Why did my webbed hands and feet go away?"

"They only come out when you're in the water," Sura said, stroking her seaweed hair. "Don't worry—you won't have to walk the halls with webbed feet!"

"Good to know . . . I wouldn't know where to get cute shoes for that."

They both giggled.

She sat up, holding the pendant between her fingers. "I also have to ask, what is the story behind this necklace? I've tried talking to Ezra and Yara, but they both said you were the only one who knew the full story."

Sura pretended to think. "Hmm . . . Nope, next question."

"Wait, what?" Ava shouted, jostling her mother's arm.

"I'm just kidding because I can see how badly you want to know," Sura said with a smile. "Of course, I'll tell you. I don't remember exactly how old I was, but I was with your father. We had just met, and we were both living at the Hadal School. The Hadal School is the underwater city of the Acathodian race and I consider it to be the most beautiful place in the world."

Ava sat back against the pillows, sighing dreamily at the thought of it. "It's hard to imagine anything much more beautiful than this place."

Sura nodded. "I thought so too when I first came here. But, anyway, your father and I were exploring the waters of the Shadow Trench, looking for a rare material we had just learned about in class."

"Fancy name, Shadow Trench. What's that?"

"Just a very deep and dangerous trench, not too far from Hadal."

"What was the material?" Ava asked.

"Trinaite," Sura replied. "It is a strong metal created from the minerals that have been fused by the heat of black smokers—"

"Black smokers?"

"Ah, yes, sorry. Sometimes I forget that you're only just starting to learn about the underwater world. Black smokers are a kind of underwater geyser. The scientific term is 'hypothermal vents.'"

"Cool."

"Though black smokers are fairly common, trinaite is hard to come by. It needs three different types of ore to bond, and this process takes a long time. Much of the known sources of trinaite had already been mined and used up, so your father and I decided to swim deep into the Shadow Trench where others did not dare to go."

"With a name like 'the Shadow Trench,' it doesn't sound like the most inviting place."

"The Shadow Trench is exactly what it sounds like—a very deep, dark rift in the ocean floor. Your father's thought was that, if we found a good-sized chunk of trinaite, we would be the richest Acathodians the sea had ever known. I was the better swimmer, so at some point I lost track of your father."

Ava grabbed a pillow from her bed and held it closely to her chest. “I thought dad was a good swimmer. He must have been if he was such a good underwater fighter.”

Sura laughed. “He was, but his decisions were sometimes a bit questionable. For instance, one time he followed a sea turtle straight into shark infested waters.”

“Yeah, that doesn’t seem like the smartest move.”

Sura continued her story. “As I swam farther into the trench, I noticed a cave. Once I was inside, glints of dim white light paved the floor, leading me deeper into the cave. I remember feeling a current caress my skin, and I could hear the faintest sound of a harp playing.”

“Sounds lovely,” Ava said.

“It really was . . .” The distant look on Sura’s face faded as she snapped back into story-telling mode. “I should mention that at this point, I could have turned back at any time.”

“What do you mean?” Ava was confused.

“The races of the sea have a saying: ‘When the Lady calls, thy soul cannot flee.’ I felt a strong urge to continue forward toward the harp sounds, but I was still in control of my own will.”

“So, at this point, you didn’t know you were being drawn to the Lady of the Lake?”

“I had no idea. I was certainly not prepared to meet her. To Acathodians, she’s practically a goddess.”

“That must have been intense.”

“The music that filled the cave was otherworldly. I could feel the water dancing around me. The lights got brighter as I ventured deeper inside, and just as I thought I was reaching the surface, there she was. She was surrounded by a magnificent aura, glowing with all the colors of the rainbow.”

Ava closed her eyes, envisioning the scene.

“As I met the Lady’s gaze, I felt calm. It was as if I had known her my entire life. She had a warm but mysterious smile, almost like the Mona Lisa’s.”

Softly, Ava said, "I've heard that anyone who finds her is never seen again."

"We have all heard the stories," Sura said. "There have been many attempts to usurp her power. Once, an army of the fiercest warriors went in search of her. Well, they finally found The Lady, but none lived to tell the tale. She is still the most feared being in the sea."

"But, Mom, if no one lived, how did anyone hear about this story?"

Sura looked uncomfortable. "They found the warriors' burned bodies. Only the Lady of the Lake is known to cause that kind of damage."

"Why do people try to kill her? Is she that evil?"

"People want her power or fear her to the point of attacking."

"It sounds like the people trying to kill her are the evil ones, not her," Ava stated.

Sura nodded. "It does seem that way, doesn't it, love?"

Ava shuddered at the thought. "Do you think she took pity on you because you were only a student?"

"No, I don't think so. Plenty of wanderers just like me were never found again. In fact, the only person ever known to escape her was . . ."

"You."

Sura nodded. "There I was, looking right into her eyes."

"What was she like? Ugly?"

"No. Very beautiful. Even so, knowing who she was, I probably should have been afraid, but I just felt this incredible sense of peace. The Lady reached out her hand, and without hesitation, I took it. Once our fingers met, I felt a charge of energy, and before I understood what was happening, I was transported back to the mouth of the cave. She hadn't said anything, but when I looked down, an ornate silver box was in my hand. I didn't know what it was at the time, but I tucked it into my utility pouch and dove back into the trench to find your dad. It was only when I opened the box later that I realized I had received a gift from the Lady of the Lake."

Ava was amazed. "So, how long did it take you to understand the necklace's powers?"

"I still don't fully understand them. So far, I only know that in stressful times it makes you faster and stronger. It can also slow down time, keeping you calm in battle. This will allow you to form a plan of attack based on wisdom rather than panic. I suspect there are many other things it can do, and now's your chance to find them."

"Thank you for giving this incredible gift to me," Ava gushed while gripping the necklace.

"Use it in good health," Sura said, smiling.

Ava was silent for a moment.

"Mom, before you go, can you tell me how you knew I was up this morning? And why could I hear your conversation so clearly?"

Sura cracked a smile. "Well, I can answer the first question. I knew you were awake because I have the greatest power of them all: motherly instinct. As to your other question, I can't say for sure. Maybe the necklace helped? I've never heard of any Acathodian having such the ability of heightened hearing, so maybe you've already found another power of the necklace." Sura gathered her daughter into a big hug. "Come on, dear, the day is passing us by too quickly."

Sura led Ava out of the room. As they walked down the winding staircase, Sura turned to face Ava.

"I left a little something in your top desk drawer."

"Thanks, mom, but you didn't have to."

"I know, but it's something I wanted you to have."

Ava and Sura stood in the lobby in front of the beautifully large entrance door. Sura took Ava's hands and gave her another big hug. Without a word, she turned and stepped outside. Ava watched the door shut behind her mother. This time, something tugged at her heart, but it was only a soft tug, not the enormous loss she'd felt, the first time Sura went away.

Instead, Ava mumbled to herself, "Well, best not to stare at a door all day," and headed off to her next class.

15

Taking Up the Gauntlet

Ava traveled down an old, curvy hallway lined with portraits and Acathodian relics, ornately carved weapons and shields and masks, on her way to Professor Lundlow's class. When she entered the class, Lundlow was already passing out blue metallic paper to each student.

Dread pooled in Ava's stomach. *Oh no. Do we have a pop quiz?*

Taking a deep breath to soothe her nerves, Ava sat at a desk with an empty seat next to it, hoping that Harper would eventually show up to fill it. Soon, the classroom was nearly at capacity, and Ava still saw no sign of Harper. Where was she? She could be lying at the bottom of the sea after having been attacked by a grindylow!

Ava paused her rattling, worried mind. Why was she fearing the worst?

Just as Professor Lundlow was about to speak, Harper ran in, breathless. Smiling sheepishly, she gave a curt nod to Professor Lundlow and went to take her seat next to Ava.

"Ava!" Harper exclaimed. "You look . . . different. I love it!"

Ava beamed, happy to see her friend, and even happier to have someone to share the experience with. "Yeah . . . I went for a swim in the ocean, and everything changed. I felt so free. For a little while, I was actually breathing underwater."

"Well, you're stunning. Even more stunning than before."

"Ladies, please quiet down," Lundlow called. "I have every intention of starting my lecture now, with or without your cooperation."

Harper lowered her voice to a whisper. "I was knocking on your door for hours. I thought you were in a coma or something."

Ava laughed softly. "I'm so sorry. I was with my mom. It's so weird. I could hear her, even when she wasn't in the room. Have you ever heard of that?"

Harper shook her head. "You have super-hearing? Wild. Why can't I be you?"

Ava laughed. "And after that, we went swimming and she told me how she got the necklace."

"Oh, do tell. And wait, you were actually able to breathe underwater?" Harper said, leaning forward with interest.

"Yeah! I was . . . I can't even explain how I did it. It just happened."

"You know that almost every student here still can't do that, right? Like, the only reason Joshua is still here is that he hasn't developed that ability yet."

"What about you?" Ava asked.

Harper choked back a laugh. "You've seen me swim. Do I look like I can breathe underwater?"

Ava laughed and turned her attention back to Lundlow's discourse.

". . . But first, everyone hold up the blue parchment in front of you. This is called tonam. Perhaps aside from strotic, the merpeople's variation of this material, tonam is the most high-tech waterproof parchment in the world."

"Merpeople suck!" a voice called out from the back.

"Hey now . . . The merpeople are our allies, and they deserve respect," Lundlow stated, giving the speaker a reproachful glance. "They have fought side by side with us in almost every war. Yes, they may be a bit arrogant at times, but they are wise and powerful."

As Lundlow continued his lecture, Harper leaned over toward Ava. "So, what did your mom have to say about the necklace?"

"Well, my dad—"

"Ladies, please!" Lundlow interrupted. "The class is in session, please focus."

"Sorry, Mr. Lundlow." Blushing, Harper sunk down in her seat and clamped her mouth closed.

Their translucent teacher gave an indignant huff. "As I was saying—"

Ava sat quietly, counting down the time so she could talk to Harper.

The bell rang, almost startling Lundlow off his desk. The class sprang up, ready to leave.

"Well, I guess that's all for today," Lundlow called after the students as they made a mad dash for the door. "And ladies, next time, please save your personal conversations for after class."

Natalie walked past the girls with two minions in tow. The oblong-faced girl standing behind her guffawed in support. Ava recognized her as Holly from her swimming class. Natalie and her friends gave their usual dirty snares, which to Ava seemed cartoonish at this point.

"Oh, how cute. I see you have your sardines following you," Harper said.

Holly growled, showing Harper her long, pointy teeth. Ava jolted backward, bumping into Harper's arm.

"Oh, what's wrong, Ava? Scared?" Natalie said with mock concern. "Well, you should be. Just wait . . ."

"I can't wait to see you cry," Natalie's other friend sneered. This girl—Ava thought her name was Olive— had an unusually long nose, and her skin was sky blue. Natalie flashed Ava a devilish grin as she and her two followers walked away.

"What was that all about?" Harper whispered once they'd gone.

Ava grumbled, "Who knows with that girl."

"So much drama." Harper rolled her eyes. "Anyway, tell me what your mother said."

As the girls made their way to Self-Defense class, Ava filled her friend in on the wonders of the morning—Shadow Trench, super-hearing, and all. When they entered the training room, Ava noticed Agatha speaking to Joshua in a corner. His eyes twinkled, and he had a huge grin on his face. Ava's second-hand excitement for him was cut short when she noticed Natalie and her two friends, giving her the stink-eye from the other side of the room. She shook it off and headed to her training station, trying to swallow her dread about what Natalie could be plotting.

"Ava!"

She turned around to see Joshua jogging toward her.

"Josh! What's up? You look happy."

"I am! And you look amazing, Ava. What happened?"

"Oh, just some crazy stuff," Ava said, unsure if her skin could even blush. She knew her old self would have, considering the way he was staring her up and down and nodding with appreciation. "So, what's up?"

"I can finally breathe underwater! Agatha took me out to sea, and we fought two grindylows and a Blue Man of the Minch. It was epic!"

"That's amazing, I am so happy for you! What's a Blue Man of the Minch?"

"They're evil blue creatures who tip over boats to drown the sailors. They don't usually come this far west . . . most are found near Scotland. In fact, I should probably bring that up with Agatha . . . Anyway, they're nasty things, with big black eyes and razor-sharp teeth."

"Yikes . . . Well, congrats on defeating one. That couldn't have been easy."

"Thanks . . . But, oh my god, Ava, I can finally breathe underwater!" Without warning, he wrapped her in a giant hug and spun her around in a circle, catching her off guard.

"A bit tight, Josh," she wheezed.

"Oh sorry." Joshua loosened his grip a bit.

Harper was quick to join in on the excitement.

"Nice job, killer!" she said, thumping him on the back.

Joshua quickly let go of Ava and stood up straight. "Thank you, thank you . . . Okay, I need to have a quick chat with Agatha, so I'll let you two get back to your sparring."

Harper leaned into her friend's ear. "Let's test some of that super-hearing, shall we? What are they talking about?"

Ava smiled. "I don't think we should eavesdrop on their conversation. Besides, I don't really know how it works. They'll tell us whatever they think we need to know."

Her friend pouted. "Ugh, you're no fun . . . Alright, I'm gonna go kick some blobby butt. See you after class."

Before Ava could find Jerzey and get to her own sparring station, a voice cut through the clamor of the room.

"I set out a challenge!" Natalie bellowed. "I challenge Ava Greene!"

The class fell silent, and all eyes turned to her. Every hair on Ava's skin stood at attention, and she looked desperately at Harper for support. Harper was instantly by her side, weapon in hand.

"Harp, what do I do?" Ava whispered.

"I don't know . . . I've never seen someone throw down like this before. But don't worry, I got your back. We can take anything she dishes out."

Ava strode over the sparring table and picked up the long knives that she had used last time. She returned to Harper's side, ready to take on Natalie and her hammer-headed friend, if need be.

"Not today ladies! Classes are canceled for the rest of the day," Agatha announced, clapping her hands, and stepping between them. "You can fight first thing tomorrow. I have an urgent matter to take care of. Weapons away, please."

Agatha left in a hurry, leaving her confused students milling about awkwardly. Joshua gingerly made his way through the crowd to Ava and Harper.

"Agatha is going to talk to Ezra about the Blue Men of the Minch. She wouldn't tell me what's going on, but I think it's bad."

"What do you mean?" Harper asked.

"Attacks on our school have been happening more often, and now enemies from around the world are on our doorstep. This is bigger than just a few random occurrences."

Carl shouted out from across the room, "We all know what's going on. War is coming! Agatha and Ezra won't admit it, but we all know. Joshua killed a Blue Man of the Minch today. What more proof do we need?"

"I've seen that kid before," Ava whispered. "He was trying to tell Ezra something along these lines when I first got here."

"Everyone thought he was crazy," Joshua said. "But maybe he's right?"

As the class dispersed, Natalie scowled at her. "Mommy dearest won't be there to save you tomorrow. I can't wait to see you crying on the floor."

Natalie's cronies sneered, sending dirty looks in Ava's direction. She was about to respond when Joshua stepped in front of them and glared at Natalie and her posse.

Fear filled Natalie's eyes, and she motioned for her friends to disperse. Without a single word, they left the room.

"Mommy dearest, my ass!" Harper shouted behind Joshua's shoulder. "She'll always have me!"

"Thanks, you guys. That was amazing." Ava put a hand on Joshua's shoulder, and he relaxed his stance.

"Thanks for what?" Harper asked.

"For defending me, you idiot."

"Any time, but you'd better be ready to take her on, she has it in for you," Harper advised.

"We should train, Avs," Joshua said.

"Avs?" Ava repeated with a smirk at Joshua.

"Too soon for a nickname?" Joshua questioned.

"Never."

Ava and Joshua maintained their gaze, smiling at one another. Tingles went down her spine.

"Also, it's nice to know that we have the best fighter in the school in our corner," Ava added, hoping she didn't shiver visibly in front of him. For a moment, everything around them seemed to fall away.

That is, until Harper stuck her face closer to theirs. "Thanks."

The moment now broken, Ava averted her gaze first and looked at her.

Harper looked suddenly off into the distance and smiled. "On that note, I'm off to eat my weight in whitefish and salmon. See ya later."

With the rest of the day free and an empty classroom to themselves, Ava thought of the perfect way to spend her extra time.

"Hey, Josh? Would you mind giving me a few pointers for tomorrow?"

He shrugged. "I don't think Agatha would mind if we borrowed a couple of her weapons for a while."

"Well, where should we begin?"

Joshua paused to think. "Seeing that you showed up halfway into the year, I doubt anyone taught you the five laws of battle yet?"

Ava shook her head.

"Alright, let's start there." Joshua grabbed a shiny blue broad sword from the training weapons table. "The first law is to end the fight as quickly as possible. That can mean a couple things: first, defeat your enemy swiftly; if that isn't an option, don't be afraid to retreat. Many people say that fleeing is cowardly, but you can't fight your enemies if you're dead."

"That makes sense. So I can run away from Natalie tomorrow?" Ava asked, only half joking.

Joshua laughed. "Are you kidding? You can't let her show you up like that!"

"Yeah, yeah, I'll try my best. What's rule number two?"

"Know that in every fight, there are always two battlefields. You fight a physical war with weapons, but there's a psychological war, too. To win any battle, you have to use your intellect."

"Which is something that Natalie is very good at," Ava interjected.

"She talks a big game. We can build a strategy around that, starting by not letting her get in your head."

Ava nodded, and Joshua went on.

"The third law is to know yourself; understand your strengths and weaknesses. Many people lose fights because they aren't paying attention to their blind spot. Consequently, it's just as important to know your enemy's strengths and weaknesses. This is the fourth law; never underestimate your opponent. If you truly understand your opponent, they will never be able to surprise you."

Ava cocked her head, trying to ignore how good he looked while he was handling his weapons with experience and ease. "Hot *dang*," she breathed as he swung the sword in a way that made him look like a superhero.

"What?"

"Huh? Oh nothing." Ava wanted to kick herself. *Did I really say that out loud?*

Joshua cleared his throat and moved on. "The final law states that to win any battle, you need to make use of your surroundings." He gestured around the room. "When you fight out in the real world, you don't have walls of weapons at your disposal, but you could easily use a rock or a fallen tree to your advantage."

Joshua pointed to two larger knives on the training weapons table. They both looked like they were made out of petrified wood. "There are no throwing knives in combat training for your level, so these are probably the closest you can get tomorrow."

Ava admired the daggers and picked them up. One was curved, while the other resembled a larger throwing knife.

"You can use both, or just one. Let's see what works best for you."

Ava swung the daggers from her fingers. Just as she was getting a feel for them, Joshua attacked. She quickly dodged Joshua's strike and retreated to a safe distance.

"Good use of law one. Now regain your ground," Joshua instructed.

Ava spun to one side and tried to surprise Joshua with an attack.

"Geez, you call that a strike?" Joshua laughed. "Natalie will absolutely win if you fight like that."

Annoyed, Ava rushed at Joshua with even more force. Once again, he casually stepped aside to evade Ava's strike.

"Law number two: you're fighting two battles at once. Don't let me get in your head, Ava. Come on, focus."

Ava took a deep breath and attempted to regain her composure. Joshua jolted forward and stopped short, making Ava take a giant leap backward. As she jabbed the curved knife in his direction, he ducked under her arm and lunged toward her once again. In a desperate attempt to evade him, Ava stumbled backward . . . only to trip over a stool and topple unceremoniously to the ground. Joshua walked over and tapped her on the shoulder with his sword.

One corner of Ava's lips tugged upward. "Law five, right?"

"Use your surroundings," Joshua said, offering her a hand.

She brushed him off and stood up on her own. "What happened to laws three and four?"

"To know yourself and your enemy takes a bit longer. Although, seeing that in this moment you are my 'enemy,' I would like to get to know you better. Maybe over dinner?" Joshua asked with an arched eyebrow.

"Smooth, Josh . . . but I don't think we're done training."

Ava attacked Joshua with a sudden swing of her throwing knife. From the expression on his face, she could clearly tell he'd been caught off guard, but he had no trouble parrying her strike.

"Not bad," he said coolly, though there was still a hint of surprise on his face. "We may make a winner out of you yet."

The two trained for hours until they were both covered in bruises. They sat down on a bench in the corner of the room to catch their breath.

"So . . ." Ava angled her body toward Josh. "Tell me something new about you."

"Hmmm . . . Well, my favorite food is sushi, I love long walks on the beach . . . Oh! And I just learned that I can breathe underwater!" A boyish grin adorned his face.

Ava laughed. "Man, you and Harper with your dating profiles. My favorite food is also sushi and I just realized I can breathe underwater, too."

He gave her an incredulous look. "Wait, hold up. What?"

"My mom came to visit this morning and we went for a swim. At first it felt so natural." Ava reached for her necklace. "Then this necklace pulled me under."

He held up his hand. "Sorry, what did you just say?"

"It was so odd. I think it was trying to help me, but no worries because here I am, and when I came up, I was changed. Like this." Ava forced a smile and waved her hands and wiggled her fingers as if giving jazz hands at a school musical.

Joshua looked confused. "And you could breathe underwater?"

"Yes! I can breathe underwater!"

"Ava, that's amazing! It takes most people years to learn that. I mean, that explains why you look different."

"Well, it'll take me years to be able to fight as well as you, so I think we're pretty even," Ava said.

They shared a long glance, until he broke it and looked up at the clock. "I should probably grab something to eat from the dining hall and head to bed."

She stood up, too. "Thanks for the training today."

"Goodnight, Ava."

When Ava got to her room, she noticed that her desk drawer was ajar. In the craziness of the day, she had forgotten that her mom had left her a gift. She removed a scroll and an envelope from the drawer and opened the letter. Seeing her mother's writing reminded her of the cute notes she used to find hidden in her lunch bag when she was just a little child.

My sweet Ava,

The necklace wasn't the only gift I received from the Lady of the Lake. Before Ryker and I were married, the Lady had a vision of your arrival and gave me a gift for you. I've never told anyone else about this, not even your father.

This scroll contains a map that I drew a very long time ago. Follow the map precisely, and it will lead you to what's rightfully yours. Bring a trusted friend or two—you may need help along the way!

I have waited so many years to give it to you, but this adventure is not mine to take. You never fail to impress me with your bravery and strength. You will need both for this journey. I love you and I'm so proud of you.

Be safe,

Mom

Ava exhaled slowly. She cleared the dust off the wrinkled map and unrolled a shiny blue parchment. Scanning the map, she immediately understood why she might need to bring a few friends; the search would lead her far off school grounds.

It was time to take Harper and Joshua on a dangerous treasure hunt.

16

THE CHALLENGE

After a nearly sleepless night, Ava woke up to a warm patch of sun that had crept onto her face. Her mind was racing with all the new things she had learned from Joshua. She had spent most of the night going over the five laws of battle, and she hoped those would be enough to defeat Natalie today. Almost all scenarios began with Natalie rushing in for the attack. Ava hoped this would be the case, as Natalie's aggressiveness could cause her to fight sloppily. If Natalie had an intricate attack plan, she would be much harder to beat.

As she sat up in bed, Ava glanced over at her mom's map. Her duel wasn't the only important thing happening today. She would have to talk to Harper and Joshua about the treasure map.

When she left her room, Harper was waiting for her in the hall.

"I was thinking about today's fight all night," Harper said, her eyes wide and a bit unfocused.

"Harper, are you okay? You look like you've had six cups of coffee."

"Nah, these are just the no-sleep jitters. But I think if we can get Natalie angry, she'll lose her cool and rush into the fight without thinking."

Ava laughed. "I was thinking the same thing at first, but she could surprise us. Maybe I'll act more afraid than I actually am and try to play into her pride."

"That's not a bad idea," Harper mused.

"When Joshua was coaching me yesterday, some of his advice reminded me of a book I read once. It's called The Art of War by Sun Tzu. He said something about how you should appear weak when you are strong, and strong when you are weak."

"Well, the second half of that sounds like Natalie for sure. She can't possibly be as mean as she lets on."

Ava grimaced. "I sure hope not. Empty threats are bad enough."

As they walked to class, Ava reflected on how lucky she was to have Harper and Joshua in her corner. She and Harper took their seats just in time to see Natalie and her posse approaching.

Natalie mouthed something that Ava couldn't quite make out.

What? Ava mouthed back.

"Ignore her," Harper whispered.

Lundlow wasted no time getting into the day's discussion. "Alright class, we have a lot to get through today, and I mean business. So, please, no side conversations."

He flashed a pointed look in Harper and Ava's direction, causing a few students to snicker.

"I'm sure many of you have heard of Isabella, the first headmistress of the Hadal School. On May 21st in 4990 BCE, she caused a massive flood to make humans pay for the destruction they had caused to the environment. Humankind was almost entirely wiped-out, except for one family that had been warned of the flood's arrival. This family allowed humans to bounce back from extinction, thus beginning what is known as the second age of Humankind."

Carl raised his hand. "Are you referring to Noah's Ark?"

"I am indeed, if that is what you choose to call it," Lundlow replied.

Excited murmurs filled the classroom.

Lundlow raised his voice over the commotion. "There were many who fiercely opposed Isabella's decision to cause the flood. Consequently, a great civil war broke out between two factions of Acathodians. It was during this war, the War of Egeria, that a warrior named Orion rose to power. He and his followers exiled Isabella and her legion from Hadal for their treachery against humans. The spark that ignited the War of Egeria occurred not far from this school. The battlefield is still littered with the ruins of this war and provides great insight into our horrifically dark past."

Naveen raised his hand. "Can we take a class trip to see the battlefield?"

"If you are all well behaved and stop trying to talk over me, then maybe we can go at the end of the semester. But, again, these are interesting, and dangerous times. We will have to hold off until we know it's safe."

The class immediately fell silent. Ava thought of the grindylows that had been seen lately near campus.

"Much better. Now, where was I? Ah, yes. The war was costly, and there were many deaths on both sides. With Isabella gone, Orion was named the new Headmaster of Hadal, due to his great wisdom and popularity. His first task was to rebuild life both on land and sea. To accomplish this, he created the Land School—a safe haven where children could learn about their history without threat from Isabella and her followers. For more than a thousand years, this school has helped countless students rejoin our people and prepare them for the challenges that we face. Maridius, the great grandson of Orion, is our current Headmaster. The bloodline of Orion has seen us through times of great discovery, and it has secured peace and prosperity for the Acathodian people."

For the first time since Ava had arrived at the Land school, the students didn't immediately clear out when the bell rang. Lundlow chuckled at his students' rapt stares as they attempted to process all the new information.

"And that is how you know you've taught a good history class. Okay, I know today gave you some big things to think about, but you have a full day ahead of you. Out you go!"

Dazed, Ava packed up her things. Ava and Harper got stuck behind Natalie and her two friends as they fanned out into the hallway.

"I can see Isabella's point," Natalie sneered.

"Yeah . . . Humans are so weak and corrupt. They're clearly inferior," Olive added.

A wave of anger bubbled up inside Ava as she thought of her human friends back in Noblesville. Ashley, Kevin, Elli. They were all twice as good as Natalie and her cronies ever would be. She dug her nails into her palms to prevent herself from saying something she might regret.

I'll deal with her in the training room. I hope.

When Ava entered the training room to see Joshua smiling at her, her anger dissipated. She focused all her attention on her upcoming fight with Natalie.

"You got this," Harper cheered.

The girls went to stand with Joshua, and the three awaited Agatha's orders. Natalie was staring Ava down from the opposite side of the room. She had tied her red and blonde hair into a bun, and was twirling a sharp, red-bladed ax, probably painted that way to symbolize blood and strike fear into opponents. Ava refused to let that work on her. She stuck to her plan and avoided eye contact. She wanted Natalie to believe that she was terrified.

"Oh, smart." Joshua's words reflected his understanding of Ava's plan.

"Two battlefields, right?" Ava whispered.

Joshua's eyes gleamed with pride, and his lips curved into a small smile.

"Alright, everybody," Agatha spoke up to draw the class's attention. "Yesterday, a challenge was thrown down. Natalie, do you still wish to challenge Ava today?"

Natalie took a step forward with her head held high. "Yes. If she's not too chicken to face me."

"I accept the challenge," Ava's voice was quiet, almost unsure. She kept her eyes fixed on the floor.

"Very well," Agatha stated. "May the best woman win. Please join me once you have picked your sparring weapons."

Ava grabbed the two long wooden knives she had used the day before and feigned bad posture as she walked to the middle of the dueling floor. The tension in the class was palpable and no one made a sound as they gathered in a circle around Agatha and the two feuding girls. Joshua and Harper made sure to stand just behind Ava as a show of their support. Agatha ushered the girls to a proper starting distance from one another. Ava turned around and locked eyes with Joshua. He gave her a quick wink, and she allowed herself to relax into her fighting stance.

"Ladies—" Agatha paused to clear her throat. "Though you are opponents now, remember that one day you will stand together to fend off our enemies."

The students started to chant the battle cry "Rok Kazock," and adrenaline coursed through Ava's body. Agatha took out her sword, and with one downward slice, the fight began.

Natalie rushed toward Ava; her wooden ax held high. Her eyes radiated pure hatred, but Ava knew that she had to remain level-headed. As Natalie came closer, Ava ducked at the perfect moment, sending her opponent stumbling past. Natalie regained her footing and crept carefully around Ava until she was within striking distance. She swung her axes with shocking accuracy, sending Ava into fight or flight mode. With a quick double attack, Natalie landed a hit to Ava's ribs.

"That's gotta hurt!" Holly jeered. "Just watch—she's going to cry any minute."

Though all the air had left her lungs, Ava braced herself for more. Josh's rules played on repeat in her head.

Seeing her opponent's weakness, Natalie quickly returned to attack mode. Ava took a shaky breath and spun past Natalie once again. This time, she landed a strike with her curved knife into Natalie's back. Natalie stumbled and clutched her lower back in pain.

"Yes, Ava!" Joshua hollered from the sidelines. "You got this!"

Natalie screamed out in frustration, which Ava took to mean she was letting her emotions get the best of her. Once she was in range, Natalie went in for another attack. This time, her assault was sloppy, but anger fueled her strikes, and each one was more powerful than the last. Ava's blades rang with each parry, and her muscles began to ache as the reverberations ran up her arms. As Natalie sped up her attack, Ava found it impossible to keep up her defense. After a series of dodges and dips, Natalie landed two crushing blows to Ava's face. Ava fell to the floor, blood dripping from her lip and ear. Agatha took a step forward, prepared to intervene if necessary.

"Ava, get up!" Harper screamed.

"You're so weak," Natalie taunted. "Stay down if you know what's good for you."

Joshua's face appeared over her, blurred and faint. "Focus, Ava. I know you can win. Just breathe."

Ava closed her eyes and took a deep breath. Instantly, a wave of calm swept through her, and she heard the slightest whisper of a woman's voice.

"Get up, Ava!" the voice whispered.

Ava gripped her knives firmly and leapt off the floor. She twisted her body in mid-air and swung the weapons at her startled rival. Ava made one last swipe, backing Natalie right up to the same stool she had tripped over yesterday. Natalie kicked over the stool and laughed. "You honestly thought I'd fall for the stupid stool trick?"

"No, I didn't . . ." Ava smiled. "*Bapalo*!"

The attack dummy's blue eyes glowed to life, focusing on its nearest target. It struck Natalie dead-on, sending her keeling to the ground. Ava launched a shattering assault, landing three powerful blows that knocked her adversary out cold. Before Ava could celebrate her victory, the attack dummy shifted its focus and came barreling toward her. As she dodged and blocked the dummy's strikes, Ava fell into a rhythmic trance. Her necklace glowed brightly, and her vision became clearer. With the last of her strength, Ava hurled her dagger at the dummy's abdomen. The automaton went flying across the room before smashing into a wall. The entire room erupted into shouts as Ava and the dummy collapsed simultaneously.

Vaguely aware of the commotion around her, Ava remained motionless on the floor. The soft voice inside her fell silent, and Ava was enveloped in darkness.

17

The Ashes of War

After what felt like an eternity, Ava's eyes readjusted to the light and focused on the ceiling above her. Joshua and Harper were looking down at her with concern, and she could hear Agatha muttering something as she tended to a still knocked-out Natalie.

"Take Ava to her room," Agatha called. "She needs to rest."

Without hesitation, Joshua swooped Ava up off the ground and followed Harper up the stairs and down the hall.

"What's the password, Ava?" Harper asked.

"Esh-my-eem," Ava murmured. As her door slowly swung open, Ava felt herself slipping back into unconsciousness. Weary from the fight, she sank into her pillows and listened to Joshua and Harper's voices growing ever more distant.

"I've never seen anything like that before," Joshua voiced.

"I think I have an idea of what happened . . . but I need to do some more research."

"What's your idea, Harper?"

"Ava's necklace was made by the Lady of the Lake. It's supposed to have magical powers, and I think we just saw one of them."

Joshua's voice was full of confusion. " . . . I need to talk to Agatha. If what you're saying is true, Ava's going to need all the help she can get. Maybe I shouldn't graduate to Hadal this year . . ."

"Joshua, why wouldn't you go? You've worked so hard, and you're finally ready."

"I know, but Ava needs me. And . . ."

"And you like her." Harper pointed out.

Joshua paused. "Yeah, I do. Let me go find Agatha. I may be able to stay, somehow. Keep an eye on her for me."

"You know I will," Harper's words echoed softly.

Ava awoke to find Harper sleeping at her desk.

"Harper," she said gently to rouse her. "What happened?"

Harper shot up and rushed to her friend's side. "You're awake!"

Ava blinked and looked around, trying to regain focus. The events of the past few hours felt like a dream. She wasn't sure what was real, and what she'd simply imagined. "I take it I lost?"

"Not at all. You knocked Natalie out cold, then the training dummy started to attack you. Let's just say, I think you may have damaged some school property."

"Wait, what? That doesn't make any sense. Natalie knocked me to the floor. Everything else after that . . ."

"Well, you got up and activated the dummy to catch Natalie off guard. Then, you battered her so hard that she got sent to the infirmary."

Ava brought her hand to her mouth. "Is she okay?"

"Yeah, she'll be fine. In fact, it was good for her. If you ask me, she needed a good ass-kicking to put her in her place."

"So . . . I won?"

"Yes, and no . . . It was kind of a draw because both of you were knocked out by the end of the fight."

Ava gnawed on her lip. "What do we do now?"

"Um . . . you slept for a whole day and a half. You should probably take it easy—"

"I can't do that. Open my desk drawer," Ava pointed.

"You shouldn't go back to class just yet," Harper warning, leaning over and opening it. "Because you'll catch hell from . . ."

She stopped as her eyes set on what was inside the drawer.

Reaching in, she pulled out Sura's map. "What's this?"

"It's a map. My mom gave it to me. I don't know where it leads, but I know we'll need some help getting there."

"What does it lead to?"

Ava shrugged. "Something my mom wants me to find. She was being mysterious about it."

"So, it's like a treasure map? That's cool. And she didn't give you any hint as to what the treasure is?"

"My mom said . . ." Ava hesitated and looked around, as if someone might be listening. She wasn't sure why, but it felt like a secret. "It's a gift from the Lady of the Lake."

Harper's mouth formed the shape of an O as Ava told her everything she had learned from her mother. When she finally made it through the story of her mother's adventures in the Shadow Trench and the Lady's premonition about her future, Harper nearly fell off the bed.

"What are we waiting for?" she cried, pumping a fist in the air. "Let's get Josh. We have a treasure to find!"

"Yes, but it takes us off school grounds, and I don't want to get in trouble."

Harper grabbed the map, gazing at it intensely. She placed her finger on one end of the map and traced along the delicate paper.

"Okay, so we start here at the school, we walk towards the forest of . . . who cares, this is a real treasure map!" Harper clapped her hands excitedly. "A treasure map given by your mother that holds a gift from the Lady of the Lake. And seeing the way your mom is such good friends with Ezra, I bet she could get you out of any trouble we get in."

Ava nodded. Harper was right. Her mother had given her this, now, for a reason. Whatever it was, it was worth the risk of getting in trouble. "I think I know where Joshua is. Follow me."

With a new rush of energy, she grabbed the map, folded it carefully, and shoved it into her pocket. Both girls ran out the door. Ava led them into the forest that stood just off the school grounds.

"Where are we going?" Harper's voice bounced with each step.

"You'll see. We're almost there!" Ava shouted back, picking up the pace.

The burbling stream grew louder as she led Harper to Joshua's clearing. As Ava had predicted, Joshua was sitting on his bench, looking into the water.

Ava shouted his name over the noise of the river.

"Ava! you're awake!" Joshua called, jumping up from his seat.

"Just wait until you hear this," Harper said. "We're going on an adventure!"

His face quickly shifted from bewilderment to concern. "Ava, how are you feeling?"

"Much better. Sit down, I have something to tell you."

The girls sat on either side of Joshua, and Ava launched into her story about the treasure that had been left for her by the Lady of the Lake. When she finished, Joshua, eyes wide, gripped the map and gazed at it, breathing a "Whoa," under his breath. His body trembled slightly, showing he was just as excited as the rest of them.

"This is unbelievable," Josh said confidently, as he analyzed the map further. He looked up and pointed through the woods, where there was a narrow, barely trodden path that rose gently before disappearing through the thick wood. "Okay, it looks like we need to go straight up that hill and then a mile or so north-east. There should be a cave there."

"We'll probably need weapons," Harper mused. "But it's not like we can waltz into the training room and borrow whatever we want."

"Well, that's not exactly true . . ." Joshua's tone offered a glimpse of hope.

They both swung their heads at him at once. He had a mysterious look on his face, like a cat toying with a canary. "Go on," Harper insisted.

"Agatha kind of lets me borrow weapons to practice with on my own," Joshua said with a smile.

Ava and Harper exchanged glances, and all three of them broke out in laughter.

Ava and Harper followed Joshua down the hall. Both she and Harper were hunched over as if sneaking down the hallway of the Louvre to steal the Mona Lisa.

"Ava, stop walking like that," Harper shouted in a whisper.

"Like what?" Ava mimicked Harper's tone and pitch.

"Like you're about to steal something," Harper answered.

"We *are* about to steal something," Ava swiftly fired back, quickly straightening. "And by the way, you're walking the same way."

Joshua calmly turned to them. "Ladies, breathe, please. Maybe I should just go about this alone?"

Harper shook her head. "No, no, we're cool, right Ava?"

"So cool." Ava leaned back, dangling her arms awkwardly, not knowing what to do with them.

Joshua turned back around and led the girls to the Self-Defense classroom.

"Make this quick," Joshua said as he grabbed his sword.

Ava stood in front of the wall with knives glaring back, the twinkle of light reflecting in her eyes. She gently brushed her fingers over the blades, aware that she was taking too much time. She needed to pick something fast. But what?

Her eyes caught on a grouping of throwing knives. Something about them called to her. *Those*. She couldn't resist taking the larger, blue-tinted knife as well.

"Ready," Ava said, running to join Joshua and Harper as she tucked her weapons beneath her hoodie.

The three hurried up the stairs and exited the school, heading back toward Josh's meditation bench. Once behind the tall trees, the three exhaled with relief.

"That's the first time I ever stole anything," Ava admitted.

Harper scoffed. "Who would've thought? You were such a ninja."

Ava laughed. "And you were any better?"

"Hey guys, you didn't steal it, you borrowed it," Joshua stated.

Joshua took the map, looked around and nodded to himself. He seemed to be having an inner dialogue Ava wished she could hear. Finally, he pointed toward a clearing. "We need to go this way."

Ava and Harper looked at each other and shrugged, and the three set off in that direction. Joshua took the lead, occasionally consulting the map. Soon, the trees dwindled in number and white sand crept onto the path. Joshua stopped suddenly to study the map more intently.

Harper wasn't looking where she was going and nearly barreled into him from behind. "Are we lost?"

"Nope, we're good," Joshua replied. He took a sharp right turn and walked on.

Ten minutes later, a chilling scream pierced the air, coming from everywhere and nowhere, all at once.

A shiver traveled down Ava's spine, and Harper spun around to look for the source of the noise. "What was that?"

Joshua gripped the hilt of his sword tightly but kept walking in the direction of the cave.

"Guys," Harper hissed. "Look to the left."

Joshua and Ava turned to see a grindylow crouching in some bushes next to the trail. The creature was foaming at the mouth. Its blood-red eyes zeroed in on the trio. Joshua let out an intimidating bellow, but the creature did not budge.

"It's preparing to attack," Joshua warned. "Stay back!"

The grindylow gnashed its pointy teeth and let out a low growl. Joshua shoved the map into his pocket and took a careful step forward, clutching his weapon tightly. The growl climbed in pitch and the creature let out another deafening shriek. When it pounced, Joshua was ready. He brandished his sword and leaped into the air to meet his attacker. The grindylow took a direct hit to the head and fell to the ground.

"Yes!" Harper shouted. "Nice!"

Joshua turned back to face Ava and Harper, but his victory was short-lived. A second grindylow was rushing at Joshua, claws stretched and ready to strike.

Ava saw it first. "Josh! Watch out!"

With a sharp flick of the wrist, Ava flung one of her knives straight at the creature's head. The grindylow screamed and collapsed into a ball, clutching its right eye. Joshua landed another blow to finish off their attacker.

Harper breathed a sigh of relief. "Nice hit, Ava, that was a close one."

"It was a bit too close. Maybe we should turn back?"

"No way, we gotta keep going," Joshua insisted. "We're nearly there."

He whipped out the map and quickly determined their path forward. Ava and Harper did their best to keep up with his quick pace. Soon, the terrain gave way to white sandy beaches so pure that they looked like they were covered in snow. Joshua slowed as they mounted a large hill. A magnificent body of water lay just over the crest.

"I don't understand . . ." Joshua said, studying the area around them. "There should be a cave or something right here."

Ava was listening intently to the breezy waves when she heard a familiar soft whisper.

"Josh, let me see that map." Ava reviewed their path on the old parchment, looking up every now and again. "I really hope I am wrong here, but I think the entrance to the cave is below us."

Josh walked to the edge of the beach. "You mean . . ."

Ava nodded as she looked at the distant waves of the ocean. "We have to swim there."

Harper frowned. "I can't breathe underwater like you two, so I guess my journey ends here. I'll keep watch to make sure nothing follows you."

Ava reached her arms out to give Harper a hug. Just then, the sound of branches cracking sent them all reeling back into attack position.

"Easy there! It's just us!"

Familiar faces appeared in the shadow of the trees.

"Seal?" Harper exclaimed.

"And Mr. Blob," Joshua added. "Man, what are you guys doing here?"

"We saw Harper and Ava run out of the school," Mr. Blob replied. "We knew you were up to something, so we followed."

"We didn't want to miss the party," Seal said with a wink.

Ava noticed that Mr. Blob had a peculiar look on his face. "Mr. Blob, what's that grin about?"

"I won my first battle." Mr. Blob grew about another foot with pride. "A grindylow attacked us while we were following you, and I saved Seal's life."

"You sure did," Seal responded, rolling her eyes. "And now be prepared to never hear the end of it."

"Nice job!" Ava's words caught her off guard. She couldn't remember exactly when her nonchalant praise turned from congratulating Russell in dodgeball, to Mr. Blob killing a sea monster. "We're happy to see you both. Joshua and I have to swim to an underwater cave— You can keep watch with Harper. She can explain the rest."

"Oh, I see. That's how you treat us non-sea-breathers, huh?" Seal said, smiling.

Mr. Blob shook his head. "The man learns how to breathe underwater, and he forgets about the little fish in the sea."

"Come on, Ava," Joshua said, offering Ava his arm. "I think we've had enough of these land-breathers."

Joshua's voice was rooted in playfulness. They all laughed. Ava looped her arm around Joshua's, and they made their way toward the water's edge.

"You okay?" Joshua asked.

"Yeah, why?" Ava took a deep breath.

"You just seem a bit tense."

"Well, the last time I swam, my necklace nearly killed me, so . . ."

"I'll make sure nothing happens to you," Joshua said, holding Ava's hand just a bit tighter.

Joshua was just trying to make her feel better, but Ava knew he couldn't save her from all things. The necklace had unspeakable power, more power than he had. Part of her wanted to take it off, but she had to believe that it was leading her toward good. After all, it had taught her how to breathe underwater.

Ava just let out a nervous laugh as her feet kept moving forward. She was happy Joshua was holding her. The treasure hunt was becoming way too real.

"I'm really happy you learned how to breathe underwater. If it weren't for your impeccable timing, I would have to do this alone."

Joshua smiled. "I'm happy to be by your side."

They waded into the water and Ava watched in amazement as Joshua shifted into his Acathodian state. His skin was light blue with white, vein-like markings. His eyes turned completely black, as if they had been clouded with oil. When Ava looked down, she saw that she had transformed as well.

"Before we go under, I have to tell you something," Joshua spoke quietly. "Mastering the ability to breathe underwater was the last thing I needed to accomplish . . . That was the last thing I needed to master before I could graduate."

Ava's heart sank. Did that mean he was leaving? After everything they'd been through? She turned to face him, trying not to let her disappointment show. "That's really great, Josh."

He looked down at the water, the small black waves rippling against their skin. His voice was quiet. "I don't have to go if you don't want me to."

Her heart twisted. Part of her wanted to insist that he stay. But how selfish would that be? "Oh, Josh. I can't ask you to stay for me."

Joshua clasped Ava's hand and she looked up to meet his gaze. "Yeah. Well. I was just thinking . . . I just met you, and I really like you . . ."

Ava put her hand on Joshua's chest. Nine months ago, she saw him for the first time, and now, they were here. Their breath in sync, swaying as one with the ocean's current. "I like you, too."

Joshua pulled Ava close. Ava could feel his heartbeat matching her own. They looked into each other's eyes and Joshua leaned in to kiss her. In the last second before his lips met hers, though, she thought of Kevin.

She pulled away.

He straightened and looked around, embarrassed. "Yeah, well . . . I guess we should go."

The couple slowly submerged and swam deeper into the sea. Faint sunlight filtered through the water and bounced off her shining skin. Once they reached the dark ocean floor, they split up and began to feel around blindly for the entrance to the cave. As her vision adjusted to the darkness, Ava noticed a large dip in the floor directly beneath her. She followed the decline for a few feet and stopped as her fingers brushed against a smooth wall. The cave was perfectly hidden. When she tilted her head slightly to the right, she could see a dark passage framed by walls that blended in with the dark waters.

"Josh!" Ava called. "I think I found it."

Joshua swam over and placed his hand next to hers, feeling for the outline of the cave's mouth. Dread crept over her, and they lingered for a moment at the entrance. Tendrils of cold water seemed to wrap around her wrists and ankles, drawing her in. Joshua seemed to be just as entranced as she.

The cave's smooth, glassy walls soon gave way to rough, rocky chambers. Massive boulders stood wedged between long pillars of turquoise calcite. Veins of gold and amethyst dust ran through the grotto, illuminating the blue-green water with a warm purple hue. Ava looked back to see Joshua using his fingernails to scratch at the walls.

"Josh, what are you doing?"

"This is real gold, Ava!"

Ava shook her head. "Haven't you ever seen Aladdin? You never touch the gold."

Joshua sheepishly moved away from the wall and followed Ava deeper into the cave. The passages appeared to be getting narrower, and soon Ava had to start swimming sideways. Just when Ava was beginning to worry that they wouldn't be able to go any further, the tunnel opened into a large chamber. They swam up to find the chamber was filled with air.

At the far end of the cavern, Ava noticed a worn wooden box standing atop a stone pillar. A feeling of guarded optimism blossomed in her chest. Years ago, her mother had hidden a treasure just for her. Had it been this easy to find all along? She pulled herself up out of the water and slowly approached the chest, ready to claim her prize. A thick metal lock with a strange keyhole caught her attention.

"Are you any good at picking locks?" Joshua mused.

"Let's find out," Ava's voice sounded with uncertainty.

Ava tried prying the lock with her knife, but the knife snapped in half.

"Nope, definitely not," Joshua said, stating the obvious.

"My turn," Joshua took his sword, raised it high and powerfully struck the lock. The sword bounced off the lock and lodged itself into the cold stone floor.

Ava acknowledged the obvious. "There isn't even a dent on the lock."

"Well, we have our answer. We need that key," Joshua stated as he pulled his embedded sword from the ground. Ava and Joshua looked around. No key would have been just lying about. Ava paused to look at Joshua. His eyes were filled with questions.

"Did your mother give you the key? Maybe you just missed it when you found the map," Joshua said.

Ava started to question if they should just return to the school, it seemed hopeless. But just as she was about to call this mission impossible off, a coy smile appeared. "She did give me the key."

She removed her necklace and stuck it into the lock, twisting the pendant until she heard a pop. Joshua watched silently as Ava lifted the lid and reached into the coffer.

She withdrew a glass flask that glimmered with an iridescent green liquid. *Drink it!* The familiar voice was louder than she remembered. Ava put the flask to her lips and gradually downed the liquid.

"Wait . . . what are you doing?" Joshua shouted.

But she couldn't stop now. After every gulp, Ava's body pulsed with a tremendous rush of power. Just as the last drop left the flask, a shockwave shook the cave.

"That didn't sound good," Joshua said.

Without hesitation, Ava snatched her necklace from the keyhole and jumped back into the water. Rocks crashed down all around them; Ava and Joshua weaved between the crumbling boulders.

Swim faster, the unknown voice whispered.

"Josh, hurry up!" she cried. Ava twisted and twirled past the falling infrastructure, moving faster than ever before. Seconds later, they shot out of the cave just before it collapsed, the whole underwater world around them shaking.

"Oh man," Joshua huffed with exhaustion. "That was close." Thick streams of bubbles floated up from his gills.

"I can't believe we made it out."

As they swam back to land, Ava sensed that she was being watched. Ava's eyes met a strange shadowy figure in the distance. A rush of fear gripped her but she held her ground and stared right back at the onlooker. Something deep inside told her that it wanted to harm her. Ava didn't take her eyes off the figure until they reached the water's surface. Both she and Joshua quickly made their way to greet the others on the beach.

"Oh, thank goodness, you're both okay!" Harper was practically in tears. "We felt this massive earthquake and, well, you were down there for so long. We were beginning to fear the worst."

"I won't lie, it was close," Joshua bent over with his hands on his knees, still breathing heavily.

"Josh, you're a bit pale. Are you alright?" Mr. Blob took a tentative step toward his friend. Ava looked over to see drops of blood dripping onto the white sand.

"Josh, turn around!" Ava's hands frantically helped Joshua angle himself for a better view of his wound. He stumbled and fell to his knees. His back was oozing blood from a deep, jagged gash.

"We have to get him back to school now!" Ava shouted.

"Wait!" Harper took charge of the situation. "First we need to apply pressure to slow the bleeding."

She ripped off the sleeve of her shirt and pressed the cloth hard against the wound. The thin gray fabric was quickly soaked through.

"It's not working!" Seal screamed.

"I have another idea. Josh . . . this is going to hurt."

Harper threw away her shirt sleeve and scooped up a couple fistfuls of sand. Joshua let out a hellish scream as Harper pressed the sand deep into his gaping gash.

"This should work to clog up the blood until we can get him back to school. Ava, Mr. Blob, you get Josh. Seal and I will run ahead to get help."

Once the four had helped Joshua to his feet, Seal and Harper took off. Ava and Mr. Blob followed slowly behind, practically dragging Joshua. As they continued forward, they heard piercing screams from a mob of angry grindylows not far behind them.

"Seriously?" Mr. Blob exclaimed. "They want to attack us right now?"

Ava readied her weapon and picked up the pace.

"Ava," Joshua croaked. "Take a sharp left by that large tree. There's a shortcut back to campus."

The teens bolted over the white sand, kicking it up in their wake. As they approached the front doors of the school, Ava saw Harper holding the door and waving frantically. They made sure to get Joshua in safely inside before they turned around. Behind them, a growing group of snarling grindylows was gathering on the beach. Ezra yanked Ava and Harper into the school.

"What is going on here?" He slammed the door shut and activated the school's warning siren.

"We were attacked," Ava wheezed. "Joshua needs help, he has a deep gash on his back."

Yara rushed over to take care of Joshua. "Who put sand in the wound?"

"I did," Harper said.

"Smart girl," Yara poured a potion into Josh's mouth and rolled him onto his side.

"Learned it from my mom," Harper said, pride seeping into her anxious voice.

Carl's voice rose above the frantic murmurs. "Why aren't the creatures attacking?"

A crowd had gathered around the bloody scene, and students were now huddling to watch through every possible window.

"Something is keeping them away." Agatha stepped forward, shooing a few students away. "What the heck did you kids get yourselves into?"

"Ezra, what should we do?" Yara asked.

"Lundlow, head to the roof," Ezra commanded. Erza looked at the other teachers and staff. "Manage the bows. We need to keep them at bay. Agatha, with me. Yara, get Joshua to the infirmary."

Ava heard the whispering voice once again. Shabar reshem. She didn't know how, but suddenly she was confident that she could stop the grindylows.

"*Shabar reshem*," Ava repeated to herself.

Ezra turned around. "Ava, what did you just say?"

In a haze, Ava calmly rose from the floor, opened the front door, and walked outside. She could feel her heart pounding beneath her ribcage, but other than that, she felt completely serene, completely at peace with what needed to be done. Her eyes smoldered with a bright blue fire, and the patterns on her skin glowed blue and white.

"What are you—Ava! Stop!" Ezra shouted.

"Ava, come back!" Harper called out.

Joshua frantically stumbled to his feet. "Ezra, we have to help her! I'm going after her."

"Sit back down!" Ezra ordered. "You're not going anywhere."

"I can't just sit here and watch!" Joshua stubbornly screamed back. Ava looked back to see her peers and the elders coming to fight alongside her. The wave of grindylows rushed forward to meet their Acathodian foes. In her trance state, Ava turned her eyes to meet the snarling creatures. She raised her arms and with an unfamiliar voice, one of power and wisdom, spoke. "Shabar Reshem!"

A shockwave blasted from her hands, scattering the grindylows across the sand. More than half of them lay dead from the impact, many of them burnt to a crisp. Ava briefly looked over her shoulder. The army of students and teachers had stopped cold in their tracks. She walked toward the few grindylows that were still alive, but they all quickly scampered back to the waves. Ava paused, standing strong as the smoke of her adversaries met the setting sun. She listened to the voices behind her.

"Did you hear what she said?" Agatha asked.

"*Shabar Reshem . . .*" Ezra repeated. There was fear in his voice.

"What does it mean?" Joshua asked.

"We stand upon the ashes of war."

18

A Fading Harp

"Are we gonna talk about what happened yesterday?"

Harper slid onto the bench across the table from Ava while she picked at her lunch. Her inquisitive gaze made Ava want to slide under the table and disappear. The overall atmosphere of the school was tense; people seemed to walk around on high alert, and there were a lot of worried whispers in the hallways. Since yesterday, there was no hiding that they were all under attack. Ava couldn't help but feel like it was partly her fault. She had gone too far off school grounds without Ezra's permission.

"I don't know, Harper . . ." Ava put her head in her hands and stared down at her plate. She no longer had the ravenous appetite she once had. "I don't know what's happening to me. The elders have me secreted away like I am some threat to all humanity."

"I know you don't, but . . ." Harper paused. "You can't blame them for being concerned. What you did was some Avatar-level stuff. No one has ever seen anything like that!"

"False," Joshua said, tossing his tray on the table.

"And good morning to you, too," Ava said, propping her chin up on her fists. "You seem like you're back to normal."

"Couldn't be better."

Harper cut in. "False? Have you seen an Acathodian do that before? I mean, even the elders looked shocked."

"Ava's ability is extremely rare, but not unheard of. I spent all night in the library trying to figure out what was going on with her."

Harper leaned forward. "What is it?"

"Um, guys? I'm sitting right here," Ava said bluntly. As much as she wanted to hear what he had to say, she dreaded it. She didn't know if she could take learning anything more about herself. "Can you stop talking about me like I have some weird disease?"

"Well, you kind of do," Joshua said. After noticing the expression on Ava's face, he quickly continued, "—but it's not an illness, it's a mutation. About sixty years ago there was a great Acathodian warrior who had the same ability."

Ava leaned forward, interested. "Well, who was he?"

"Here's the crazy part: no one seems to know. This book had the whole nine yards on every great Acathodian leader and warrior, but for some reason, this person was left anonymous."

"Maybe it was to protect his identity," Harper suggested. "I know I wouldn't want to become public enemy number one for Isabella."

Joshua shot Harper with a dubious look. "Anyway, the good news is that you have a very rare and very cool ability."

"Thanks, but I'm going to have to learn how to manage it better. I'm still drained from yesterday. Why me? Why am I the only one who can—"

"We all have our own abilities. Mine is super strength," Joshua replied. "It's not quite as awesome as being able to smite your enemies on the battlefield with a single look, but it's something."

"How about you, Harper?" Ava asked.

"I don't have one yet. Abilities develop after you learn to breathe underwater."

"Oh. Well, what special power would you choose if you could?"

"I guess I would want to control electricity," Harper said. "Like an electric eel."

"I hope that works out for you, Harp," Joshua said. "I wanted to be able to turn invisible, but clearly the universe had other plans."

Ava cocked her head to one side. "Wait, Acathodians can actually do that?"

"Yeah, pretty much. Some are connected to different kinds of octopuses, so they can blend in perfectly with their environment."

"Octopi," Harper confidently stated.

"What?"

"You said octopuses, it's octopi."

Joshua laughed. "Tomato, tomahto. I didn't know you were such a stickler for grammar."

Ava grabbed her tray and rose to her feet. "As much as I hate to break up your squabbles, we're going to be late for class at this rate."

"Shoot, you're right!" Harper gobbled down the last few bites that remained on her plate.

"Josh . . . I'll see you later?" Ava asked as Joshua smiled and walked away.

Ava held Joshua's gaze for a few extra seconds.

"Well, I may not have the ability to electrify, but it seems you both do," Harper said, adding a quick laugh. Ava smiled, this time not putting up much of a counter argument. Ava could no longer deny reality, her reality. Harper was quick to dissolve the mood. "Okay we have to go; we don't want to keep Yara waiting."

The girls put away their trays and sped off to the pool. They mulled over the previous day's events and somewhere along the way, they dissolved into fits of uncontrollable laughter. Everything seemed so surreal. Laughing about it seemed like the only way to cope, and Ava was happy to loosen up with her best friend. They entered the classroom to find Yara going over the day's schedule. Ava was unsurprised to see Natalie and her goons already getting in their dirty looks for the day.

"Jump in, Harper." Yara looked deep into Ava's eyes. "Ava, with me." Ava and Harper shared a quick and worried gaze. Ava walked slowly towards Yara; her ears as focused as her eyes awaiting Harper's entrance into the pool. Harper splashed in elegantly.

"Yes, Yara?" Ava's voice was blanketed with worry.

"The elders and I are concerned about you."

"About my ability? I am sorry if I did something wrong." Ava's apology was also spoken as a plea. Was she going to be kicked out of school? Forced to be a lab rat, or exiled?

"Not exactly. It's your ability to speak an ancient tongue that has us . . . confused." Yara was clearly choosing her words wisely.

Ava just stood still, she knew hearing voices in her head was never a good thing; ironically, Ava's own words couldn't make it past her lips. Yara bent just slightly towards Ava, eyes locked to her necklace. With the slightest of hmms, Yara straightened her posture once again.

"Let's just have fun today, we all are under so much stress these days. Go join Harper, Ava." Yara's voice sounded forced. It was almost as worrying to Ava as Yara's stern voice.

Ava slowly turned away from Yara and walked towards the pool, where Harper was waiting. Once Ava leaped into the pool, her mind was free from all stress. The water seemed to wash away her worry. Then she noticed a vast assortment of obstacles laid out in a winding maze under the water. Some of the obstacles moved while others remained stationary. Following Agatha's instruction, Ava and Harper dove deeper into the pool and took turns navigating their way through each of the challenges. When they arrived at the end of the maze, they came across a narrow tunnel. Peering inside, Ava recognized a locus-spiked plant near the entrance. Winding stems covered in six-inch thorns radiated out from the central bud, lining the inside of the tunnel. Ava gathered her courage and slowly made her way into the prickly den. Though she was ever so careful not to make any sudden movements, there were times when the thorns came millimeters from slicing into her skin. When Ava triumphantly exited the tunnel, she noticed that her friend was no longer behind her.

"Harper!" she yelled into the darkness. Minutes passed, and Ava began to feel frantic. Just as she was about to go back inside, she began to make out Harper's bright blue head at the far end of the tunnel.

"Are you okay?" Ava shouted. When Harper finally emerged from the thorny tunnel, she pointed to the sky and swam to the surface to pop her head out of the water. Ava rushed upward to meet her.

"Sorry," Harper said. "I couldn't respond because I was busy holding my breath. Not all of us can breathe underwater, remember?"

"Right, my bad."

"Anyway... Look what I found!" Harper held up a large copper coin.

Ava swam closer to get a better look. "What does it say?"

"Collect a gift from Yara." She directed her attention to their teacher. "Yara, I found this coin."

"Wonderful! I hid that coin two years ago."

Harper grinned. "Sweet! Do I still get a gift after all this time?"

"Yes, of course! Hold on for just a minute while I go get it."

Yara walked to her office and returned with a gold-plated trophy that had to be at least three feet tall. Harper hauled herself out of the pool and ran over to give Yara a big wet hug.

"This is my first trophy ever!"

"You've earned it. It is one thing to find treasure when you are told to open your eyes, what you did was much more difficult. You had your eyes open from the start, and because of that, you found treasure. Congratulations, Harper." Yara carefully extracted herself from the soggy embrace.

"Aw look," Natalie said, feigning her voice dripping with mock sincerity. "Little Harper won a trophy for not dying."

"Hey!" Yara snapped. "If you keep up that tone you will be spending the rest of today mopping the locker room floor. I will not tolerate trash talking in my class."

Harper and Ava exchanged glances. Yara was scary when she was angry.

She huffed and wandered to the edge of the pool. "Alright everyone, that's enough fun for today. Line up in your groups—we're racing."

The class gathered quickly at the far side of the pool.

"Good luck, Harper," Ava said.

"You too," she responded. "Smoke her!"

Ava headed to her line to face off with Natalie. Natalie was already scowling in her direction, but this time Ava didn't hesitate to glare back.

"I know you're going to lose, but I can't wait to see Harper's face when—"

"When what?" Ava retorted. "I'm getting fed up with your empty threats."

Natalie snickered. "You'll see."

Ava rolled her eyes and focused her attention on Harper. She was engaged in a heated conversation with Natalie's shark-like friend. A slender boy with green swirls on his skin approached Ava. "The shark girl—Holly—is a nightmare. Olive—the blue one who looks like a dolphin—is crazy, but super basic. She's pretty much all talk and no action."

Ava laughed. "Your name is Logabet, right?"

"My entire life," Logabet said.

"What an interesting name."

"Yep. My parents have a bit of a flair for the dramatic. I guess so do I, am I right?"

Ava laughed. "Never a bad thing."

Logabet said, "Apparently, I am not the only one who has a bit of a dramatic flair."

Ava laughed. "Well, that's why we will be such good friends."

A sharp voice cut them off. "Can you two losers go away?" Natalie barked. "You're taking up my air."

Logabet sighed and crossed his arms. His skin shifted from purple and green to yellow with black stripes "If only . . ."

"Woah, you just changed color!" Ava exclaimed. "That's awesome!"

"Yeah, it's the only ability I've been able to hone so far. And a good party trick."

Natalie huffed and walked away.

"Are you sure you don't have any other abilities?" Ava asked.

"No, why?"

"Well, you just got Natalie to stop talking. That's pretty impressive."

"Ooh, someone's feeling sassy today," Logabet said, laughing. "Somebody has to tell her off—she's awful."

Yara's voice cut their conversation short. "Kol Levs, you're up first! Natalie, you won last time, so you get to pick your opponent."

"Well, it's not like anyone is going to be very hard to beat, but I will challenge—"

"I'll race her!" Logabet interrupted, raising his hand.

"This is Natalie's decision," Yara insisted.

". . . Ava," Natalie finished.

"Surprise, surprise," Ava muttered.

"Of course," Logabet replied. "Because you know you would lose if you raced me."

"Oh please! You're completely useless," she hissed. "All you do is turn pretty colors, you're just a useless rainbow flag who hasn't any real abilities."

Logabet set his jaw and clenched his fists. "At least I'm not a heartless bigot like you."

After a tense silence, Yara called for Ava and Natalie to get into racing position. Ava planted her feet on the smooth, wet marble and bent down. She took a deep breath and turned all her energy toward winning the race.

"*Yatza*!" Yara shouted.

Ava leapt into the war with as much power as she could muster. The water seemed to morph around her. She glided with ease as though she were riding an air current, but continued to thrust forward to increase her lead over Natalie. Before she knew it, her hand touched the other side of the pool and the race came to an end. Ava smiled and giggled to herself. It's so much easier to swim when you can breathe underwater. When she turned around, she realized that Natalie was nowhere to be found in the pool. In confusion, she looked around the rest of the room, scanning her classmates' faces.

"Where's Natalie?" she asked. "Did she beat me?"

"Not at all," Harper replied with a sly smile. "She saw just how fast you were and dropped out of the race halfway."

Just then, Natalie came back into the room, still dripping, a towel around her waist. "Sorry, Yara. I forgot I left my water bottle in my room."

"Natalie, you got wrecked!" Logabet taunted. "What a sore loser! You couldn't even finish the race."

Yara pressed her lips together, choosing to ignore the taunting. "Nice job, Ava. Okay, Harper and Logabet—"

"I challenge Harper!" Holly shouted.

"Interesting," Yara said.

Harper and Ava exchanged nervous glances. Something weird was going on.

"I want to test into the Kol Levs swim group and challenge Harper," Holly said, speaking louder this time.

Yara nodded hesitantly. "Those are the rules . . . If you can swim a lap in under two minutes, I will let you into the Kol Levs group."

Holly readied herself at the edge of the pool. When Yara called for her to start, she took off with alarming speed. She made it all the way to the opposite end of the pool without lifting her head from the water.

"Is she breathing underwater?" Ava whispered.

"I think so," Harper replied through gritted teeth. "Oh lord, I'm screwed."

"One minute and fifty-eight seconds," Yara said once Holly had completed the lap. "Congratulations, Holly, you are now in the Kol Levs group."

"Oh, hooray. . ." Holly said, smirking as she lined up next to Harper. Ava looked on with concern. This didn't feel right.

"*Yatza*!"

The girls dove into the pool. At first, the race was tight. But as Harper started to take the lead, something happened.

A sickish green cloud seemed to emanate from Holly's body, quickly spreading through the pool. Ava watched in horror as the green miasma quickly engulfed Harper.

Before long, neither girl was visible in the pea-soup colored mixture.

Natalie cackled from the sidelines while Holly swam to the finish, putting up her hand first. Ava ran to the edge of the pool looking for Harper, but the foggy green substance was difficult to see though.

Yara rushed over as well and shot Holly a look of pure anger. "What was that?"

"Oops," Holly said smugly. "I guess I don't know how to handle my ability yet."

Yara turned her attention back to locating Harper. The surface of the pool was absolutely still. Ava looked over at Holly celebrating with Natalie and Olive. The three of them were cheering as if Holly had won fairly. As the seconds ticked by and Harper did not emerge, Ava knew something was really wrong.

"Harper!" she shouted at the pool. "Where are you?"

Yara looked back at Ava with wide, worried eyes. Without faltering, Ava dove into the poisonous water. As she took her first few strokes, it quickly dawned on her what Harper had been through. The green toxin made it impossible for Ava to breathe. Ava once again found herself holding a single breath.

But it only got worse. As she swam deeper, looking desperately for her friend, her skin and eyes started to burn. As the pain increased, Ava could not help but let out a cry of agony, but with that, she lost her most precious breath. Her lungs deflated, and she started to gasp. Yet she never lost her stroke; Ava would not let Harper die today.

Ava pushed harder through the water, trying to move the deadly sludge away from her with each stroke. She frantically felt her way through the thick fog, until her hand collided with something solid at the bottom of the pool. Harper. In her panic, Ava's skin started to radiate a bluish hue and her eyes shone white.

The whispering voice returned. "*Klor my-eem*."

Ava had no air to breathe, let alone to speak, but out of desperation, she mouthed the ancient words. The water instantly started to clarify once again as the toxic liquid vanished. Ava heaved in a breath from the clear water, feeling her lungs open, the toxins releasing from her body. Wasting no time, Ava grabbed her friend and dragged her lifeless body back to the surface.

Yara and some students helped heave Harper's body over the lip of the pool. Scrambling up the side, Ava rolled her friend over on the tile floor and tried to shake her awake. "Wake up, Harp! Please, wake up!"

Yara jumped to her feet and ran to her office.

"Just try to breathe . . ." Ava whispered in Harper's ear.

Yara rushed back to Harper's aid, holding a crystal bottle filled with black liquid. She poured the mysterious brew into Harper's mouth. Harper's skin began to turn waxy and pale.

Ava tried to keep herself calm, but it was hard to keep her hands from shaking. "Yara, what's happening? She doesn't look good."

"She's fading fast," Yara said.

Logabet came rushing into the room with the Acathodian doctor. The doctor ran to Harper's side with his kit.

"Can you save her?" Ava whispered, her heart beating madly.

The doctor did not respond. He took out a glass flask with the same black liquid that Yara had given to Harper.

"I used mine already," Yara said. "It did nothing."

The doctor fumbled in his bag for another potion. This time, he took out a flask with a clear liquid. As he was about to pour it into Harper's mouth, she awoke, coughing up slimy green goo. Harper's skin slowly regained its normal brown hue, and her eyes brightened. She reached for Ava's hand, gently pulling her closer.

"Push me in the water," she whispered.

"Um, that doesn't seem like a good idea," Ava replied. "You weren't breathing."

Harper rolled herself out of Ava's grasp and flopped back into the pool, now clear of any toxin.

Confused, Ava dove in after her. She caught sight of her underwater, stroking easily through it. When Harper turned back, she gave her friend a thumbs up, then laughed with glee as a rush of bubbles escaped from her nose.

Harper was breathing underwater.

19

What's the Message?

As the sun peeked through Ava's window the next morning, she relished the feeling of relative normalcy it brought her. No matter how hectic her world was, the sun would always rise. Humming a joyful melody, she rolled out of bed and dressed for the day. Ava continued her morning song all the way down the winding staircase and to the dining hall. There, she spotted Harper and Joshua talking. Harper was wildly flinging her hands at a saltshaker. Ava furrowed her eyebrows and sat down next to her.

"Harp, you okay?"

"She's trying to electrify the saltshaker," Joshua explained.

Harper stopped her hectic hand gestures. "Guess that's not working."

"Well, it certainly wasn't from lack of trying," Joshua said.

Harper let out a defeated sigh. "What if I don't have a special talent?"

"I'm sure you do," Ava encouraged. "You just haven't found it yet."

"Well . . ." Joshua paused. "Not every Acathodian develops an ability. Though it's rare not to."

"Jeez, Josh, don't freak her out!" Ava shot him with a disapproving look and turned to Harper. "You're bound to have a special talent hidden in there somewhere. You're too awesome not to. Just be patient with yourself. You only started breathing underwater yesterday."

Harper smiled half-heartedly. "Thanks, Ava. Well, if we're ever going to find my awesome ability, we certainly aren't going to do it here, stuffing our faces. Let's go to Agatha's room."

When the three arrived, Agatha was reading a paper at her large wooden desk.

"Agatha?" Harper asked. "Can we use the training room to test something out?"

Agatha flapped her hand in approval without looking up from her paper. Joshua stood by in anticipation as Ava led Harper over to the attack dummy. Standing in her battle stance, Harper nodded to Ava to signal that she was ready. Ava's voice jolted the dummy to life, and it propelled itself at Harper, sword in hand. Harper dodged and leapt past each violent swing.

"Try to blow venom at it," Joshua suggested.

Harper began spitting at the dummy to no effect. "It's not working!"

She wiped the drool from the sides of her mouth and jumped out of the way as the dummy swung at her yet again.

Joshua chuckled. "It was worth a shot. Hmm . . . Maybe try to shoot spikes out of your hands?"

Harper flung her hands forward, but nothing happened. She tried again, and again without success.

"Nothing is working," she said frantically. "I just feel ridiculous!"

"Wait, I got it!" Joshua shouted in excitement. "Try using sonar!"

Harper started to hum different off-pitch notes that sounded more like shrieks than melodic sounds.

Ava grimaced. "Okay, definitely not sonar."

"Let's just stop." Harper dodged another attack. "This is a waste of time."

A loud and commanding voice shouted from the back room, turning the dummy off.

"Just FYI, sonar works best underwater!" Agatha called. "But let me assure you all that sonar is not Harper's ability. That was absolutely ear-piercing."

"Thanks, Agatha," Harper said sarcastically.

"Any time." Agatha smiled. "Don't be upset Harper. You will find your ability."

"Yeah, she's right. You'll probably figure it out when you're least expecting it," Ava said.

Agatha nodded. "It's also possible that you've already used your ability and you just didn't realize it. Abilities often feel so natural that you may have missed it."

"I think I would know," Harper said. "I feel the same as always, except that I can breathe underwater now."

"Why don't we go to the pool?" Ava proposed. "We can try out other ideas in the water."

"Sounds good," Harper replied. "Let's meet there in ten minutes."

Ava ran down the hallway and up the curling stairs to her room. When she walked in, Sura was sitting on her bed. Ava's face lit up and she ran to hug her mother.

"Mom, what are you doing here?"

"Ezra called me. He said that you've developed some interesting abilities and that you've had a few close calls with our enemies. I convinced Ezra not to punish you all, as it was mainly my fault to send you there in the first place."

Ava laughed. "The grindylows were an unexpected part of the treasure hunt. But I don't think I have just any ability. Joshua and Harper think that what I can do is extremely rare. I burnt a bunch of grindylows to a crisp by shooting lightning or something from my hands."

"That is rare indeed," Sura said. "But it's not what I was talking about."

"It's not?"

"Not exactly. I was alarmed when Ezra told me some other things."

"What did he say?" Ava said.

"Right before you lit the grindylows on fire you spoke an ancient Acathodian dialect. A language you can't possibly know; it has not been spoken in over five thousand years."

Ava paused. "Mom . . . I hear voices in my head. A woman whispers things to me."

"Go on," Sura prompted, surprised.

"Whenever I get into trouble or I need help, I repeat the words this woman tells me. Am I going crazy? I thought it was just another ability."

Sura hugged her daughter tightly. "You're not crazy, Ava."

"So, is zapping people not my ability after all?"

"Ezra is still trying to figure things out, but there is nothing wrong with you," Sura assured as she hugged Ava tightly.

After a brief silence, Ava spoke again. "I found the treasure. I don't know what that potion was, but the voices have been louder since I drank it."

Sura stiffened. "Is that true?"

Just then, a loud knock sounded on Ava's door. Ava said the password and the door swung open to reveal Harper in her swimsuit. Harper's eyes brightened, and she rushed past Ava to give Sura a hug.

"Harper," Sura said, seemingly pleasantly surprised by Harper's affections.

"How are you, Sura?"

"I'm well, Harper. And you?"

"I can breathe underwater now," Harper said proudly.

"I could tell something was different about you. That's fantastic!"

"Ava and Joshua have been trying to help me discover my ability," she continued. "We were just about to head down to the pool to see if I had any underwater abilities."

"Don't push yourself too much, Harper. You will find your ability in due time. Try not to force it. Also," Sura smiled and dropped her voice to a stage whisper. "What's going on between Ava and Joshua?"

"Oh, they're definitely a thing," Harper said, grinning.

"Would you look at the time?" Ava exclaimed, pretending to look at a watch she wasn't wearing, then. nudging her friend toward the door. "Harper, we should go."

Just then, a loud bell sounded, unlike anything Ava had heard before, the vibration was enough to rattle the walls. Sura jumped into high alert while Ava and Harper looked at each other in confusion. "What is that?" Ava asked.

"Quickly," Sura said, her eyes darting about as she led the girls to the main entrance. When they reached it, Ava saw a group of students already gathering at the windows. Joshua rushed out of the crowd to join his friends. Ezra was already outside greeting a tall woman in bronze armor.

"That is a messenger," Sura explained.

"Yeah, but what's the message?" Ava asked, gazing at the beautiful woman.

The Acathodian messenger entered the school, chin up, with a regal bearing. She stared straight ahead, not making eye contact with anyone. The students parted like the Red Sea so that she and Ezra could pass. Ezra turned around to face the students and raised his arms to get everyone's attention.

"Students, classes are canceled for the rest of the day. Please return to your rooms for the time being, and then you may continue your day as planned. We will hold an assembly tomorrow morning to discuss this further."

No one uttered a word as he and the messenger disappeared into his office. Ava saw her mother mouth a few words to Yara. *This can't be good.*

20

MOVING ON BUT NEVER FORGETTING

Awaiting news from Ezra and the Acathodian messenger, Ava, Joshua, and Harper retired to Ava's room. An eerie silence swept through the halls, and the high tension crept in through the cracks under and around Ava's door. The entire school was on edge and Ava could not sit still.

"How long do they need us to stay in our rooms?" she blurted out.

"I don't know, but all this sitting is making me tired," Harper said through a yawn. "I'm going to my room for a power nap but let me know when your mom gets back from that meeting. I can't believe Sura barged in there like that."

"Yeah," Ava said. "I would have loved to see Ezra's face."

After hugging Harper goodbye, Ava turned around to find Joshua admiring the pictures on her wall.

"These are awesome. How old were you here?"

Ava laughed. "Oh gosh. I think I was twelve in that one. That was my first time going to New York City. It felt like a completely different world."

"I bet. Kind of like being here."

"It's a bit more spacious here, but equally as chaotic. Here we have grindylows, there you have giant rats," Ava joked. Ava looked at Joshua. "Let's get out of this room. We can go to your spot by the river."

Joshua looked at Ava with wide eyes. "I don't know, Ava. That could be dangerous."

Ava's lips curled into a mischievous smile. "There's a thin line between danger and fun. What do you say?"

"You're difficult to disagree with. Especially when you're looking at me like that."

Ava led Joshua out of the room and down the stairs. When they reached the front entrance, they quietly opened the door and peeked outside. Seeing that the coast was clear, the two ran toward the river. The sun was desperately trying to shine through the gray clouds while the trees shed their colorful leaves onto Ava and Joshua's heads. They soon found their way to the wooden bench.

After a few moments, Ava broke the silence. "It is so beautiful out here."

Joshua smiled and looked into Ava's eyes. "Indeed, it is."

"Josh, I'm really happy that I met you."

"Same here, Ava. You have no idea."

Joshua clasped his hands together and looked down at his lap. His leg was bouncing with nerves. "I want to tell you something. Something I've never told anyone before."

Ava put her hand on his knee, hoping to comfort him. Joshua took a deep breath and turned to face Ava, holding her gaze. "Okay?".

"When I was five years old, my mother passed away. She had tuberculosis and it just got out of control. After that, my stepfather was never able to function without a drink in his hand. To make things worse . . ."

Ava traced small circles on his hand. When he had collected his thoughts, Joshua continued.

"I was also having trouble in school. Everyone thought I was stupid, and for a long time I thought I was, too. My stepfather started yelling at me. He would call me names . . . And then he resorted to hitting me, as if he could beat the wisdom into me.

"I wanted to run away. I wanted to drop out of school and start over. I couldn't escape my stepfather at home and going to school was a nightmare. The kids laughed at me because I couldn't read as quickly as them. I got bullied because I couldn't spell, and my teachers would call me lazy because they thought I wasn't motivated or that I was 'acting out.' Of course, this just made my stepdad lash out more."

Ava moved closer and gave his hand a squeeze. "Joshua, I am so sorry."

"Then, one day, I started to change. I had no idea what was happening to me. But that night, something miraculous occurred. A strange-looking man knocked on my door and said that he would take me in."

"Who was he?" Ava asked.

Joshua smiled. "Ezra."

Ava looked at Joshua with tears in her eyes. "He saved you."

"In so many ways. He introduced me to life as an Acathodian, and to this day he still treats me like his son. He taught me how to read, write, spell, fight, and swim. Most importantly he made me see how smart I was. I'm not stupid, I just have a learning difference: dyslexia."

"Joshua, you're one of the smartest, most caring guys I know."

"You mean it?"

Ava nodded.

The pair spent hours talking and getting to know each other better. Ava told Joshua about her old school and about Kevin. She realized that she felt more at home, here with Joshua, than ever before. Eventually, they noticed that the sun was fading.

"We should go back," Ava said. "I have no idea what time it is, but people are probably going to start looking for us soon."

"Your mom?"

"I actually meant Harper," Ava said, laughing.

When they returned to the school, Ezra and Sura were waiting in the lobby with worried expressions on their faces. They shot up from their seats and rushed over.

Ezra was fuming. “What part of ‘go to your rooms’ did you not understand, Joshua?”

Joshua stiffened. “I’m sorry, sir.”

Sura placed her hands on Ava and Joshua’s shoulders. “You two better go meet Harper in the dining hall. She was looking all over for you. We’re about to make a schoolwide announcement. See you there shortly.”

“Something tells me bad news is coming,” Ava mumbled.

As if to confirm it, they entered the dining hall and saw Harper sitting with arms crossed and a grumpy face.

“Speaking of . . .” Joshua trailed off as they sat next to her.

“Harp, you okay?” Ava asked.

“First thing: Don’t act like I didn’t see you two holding hands like the cutest couple ever. But that’s not going to make up for you guys ditching me.”

Just then, Ezra, Sura, and the Acathodian messenger entered the room with the rest of the elders. Everyone fell silent.

“Something is definitely wrong,” Ava observed. “Ezra looks shaken to the core.”

Ezra took center stage and inhaled deeply before he spoke. “My dear students, I have some news from the Hadal School. There is no good way to say this, so I will just come out with it. There have been a number of horrible attacks on Hadal, and we have lost many loved ones there. Despite all that has transpired, the school still stands. We must stay strong and united in these dark times.”

A girl with piercing gray eyes and long brown hair stood up. “Ezra, my mother . . . Is she okay?”

Ezra looked at her in defeat. He seemed to age twenty years in the span of a few seconds. He glanced at Yara for help, and she quickly walked over to comfort the girl.

"I am so sorry, my dear," Ezra said.

"No!" The girl fell to her knees and began to weep. "Not my mom . . ."

Ava clasped a hand over her mouth in horror, tears springing to her eyes as two of the girl's friends huddled around her on the floor and hugged her tightly. Yara joined them and rubbed the girl's back, whispering words of comfort. When she was ready, Yara helped the girl up and escorted her and her friends out of the dining hall.

Ezra cleared his throat and mustered the strength to continue. "Due to the brutal attacks on Hadal and our family, we are holding an early graduation. Many of you will have to leave this school and go defend Hadal."

Anxious murmurs filled the dining hall.

"What does this mean?" Ava asked.

"It means . . . I have to leave," Joshua said quietly.

The Acathodian Messenger took center stage. "I know this will be tough for all of you. It is never easy to leave your home and your friends behind. But you have another home, another family. A family that loves you and needs you now. I will be leaving with the graduates tomorrow."

The students descended into chaos. Many of them were in tears, others shouting and proclaiming their loyalty. Some were filled with rage, ready to avenge their fallen family members. Ava stood silent, frozen, trying to comprehend what this meant for her and her friends. She couldn't help thinking of that moment with Josh, by the river. It was such a sweet, tender moment, and now, it seemed so long ago.

Everything was different now. Absolutely everything. They were at war.

Ezra spoke once again. "Although this is unexpected, we will keep our traditions alive. You will carve your names into the walls of this school as we do every year. Future students will know of your bravery and tell tales of the Acathodians who lived here and made this school strong. Tomorrow, we move on, but we will never forget our past."

Sura stood tall next to Ezra. "I will now announce the names of the students who will be graduating tomorrow and continuing their journey to Hadal."

Sura unfurled a long scroll of blue parchment and began to read a list of names. Each student had a different reaction. Some nodded bravely, some cried, but everyone accepted their duty with honor.

"Leon, Carlton, Victoria . . ." Sura's list seemed endless. "Olivia, Weathers, Jimmy R. . . ."

"Jimmy R? That's Mr.Blob!" Harper whispered.

The names continued. "Seal . . ."

Ava clenched her teeth as each name was read off. "All of our friends are leaving."

Sura continued. "Naveen, Maya . . ."

Maya was the young woman who had just lost her mother. She stood in the doorway, her eyes now dry.

"Good, let them know I'm coming!" she called. "Those monsters took my mother from me, and I will take their miserable lives from them."

"I feel so bad for Maya," Harper whispered.

"I can't believe we're going to war again," Joshua murmured.

"Mia, Emma, Hathor . . ."

Joshua looked over at Hathor. He smiled and pumped his fist.

"Rio, Amelia, Noah," Sura paused, then said the name that Ava had been expecting, but dreading "Joshua . . ."

She looked over at him, tears springing to her eyes. "It's okay," Joshua said, taking her hands in his. "I'm honored to go. There are so many people who need my help there."

A lump welled up in Ava's throat. "Why couldn't they take Natalie instead . . ."

"It's all the upperclassmen. It's just a year or so. Both of you can breathe underwater, if you work hard, you can graduate in the year," Joshua said, sounding older than he had, only moments ago.

Joshua drew Ava and Harper into a group hug. When the three of them let go, Ava wiped her eyes. "I'll be waiting for you. Then we'll never have to say goodbye again."

Hathor approached the group hesitantly. "Hey Ava, I know this wasn't the way you wanted things to go, but I will take care of Joshua for you. I promise I won't let anything happen to him."

"Thank you, Hathor," Ava said.

He gave her a curt nod, and then clapped his friend on the back. "Come on, Joshua. We need to get our things ready for tomorrow."

"I know." Joshua didn't look away from Ava, even as Hathor escorted him out of the dining hall.

21

Graduation

Ava spent the night tossing and turning, fighting to fall asleep as her mind raced with thoughts of Joshua's departure. Eventually, she gave up on resting and gazed through the window at the moon's reflection, rippling over the dark crests of the water. Stars dazzled the night sky with their brilliant twinkle. Ava watched as they faded into nothingness with the rising sun. As the first birds began to sing, she got out of bed, dressed, and journeyed to the roof. She found her mother there, already taking in the morning. Ava approached quietly and sat down beside her.

"I know you're sad, minnow," Sura said softly. "But this isn't such a bad place to wait out the year."

"It seems like I'm always being forced away from people I care about. First Kevin, now Joshua . . . I don't even understand why he needs to leave." A hint of anger crept into Ava's voice.

Sura sighed. "I should have told you our people's history long before I brought you here. There has been an ongoing war that dates back thousands of years. This power struggle has caused the other side to use terror tactics to hurt and kill our people. Sadly, this is the life we live."

“I get that,” Ava said. “And trust me, I’m happy to help and do my part. But I just wish we could have gone together!”

“I know, sweetheart.”

Ava and Sura sat quietly until the sun was fully up. When the sounds of stirring students and elders began to waft up from the halls, Ava spoke.

“Even though I’m not in the best mood today, I want to be there for Joshua and my other friends. This is a big day for them.”

Sura hugged her daughter. “I’m sure they will all love to see you at the ceremony.”

Once they were downstairs, they found Joshua standing in the lobby, scanning the area thoughtfully as if trying to commit it all to memory.

“I think I should leave you two to talk,” Sura whispered, nudging her forward and turning to head down the hallway.

Ava crept up next to Joshua and the two stood in silence. Ava followed his gaze to the ornate carvings on the doorframe.

Joshua broke the quiet. “I can’t believe I’ve spent just shy of a decade here. This place is the only real home I’ve known.”

Ava smiled sadly. “But just think soon you’ll be in a new home. Lundlow always says that Hadal is even more beautiful than the Land School. I’m sure you’ll love it.”

Joshua nodded absentmindedly. “I always looked forward to joining our people at Hadal . . . But that was before I met you.”

“Like you said, if I work hard, I may be able to join you in a year or so.” Ava knew she had to be strong. “When I graduate, you can show me around Hadal, just like you did here.”

Joshua gave Ava a soft kiss on the cheek. “That sounds great.”

“Hey, kids,” Ezra whispered, his voice trembling with a mix of anticipation and nostalgia. He approached slowly, his steps laden with the weight of memories, his golden sword glimmering by his side like a beacon of a forgotten era.

"Hey, Ezra," Joshua replied softly, his eyes fixed on the ground. He sensed the gravity of the moment, the unspoken emotions that swirled in the air.

"Joshua," Ezra began, his voice quivering with affection, "when I knocked on your door all those years ago, a surge of hope overwhelmed me. In that instant, I knew deep in my heart that our destinies were forever intertwined, that we would become family." Ezra's voice cracked with emotion, revealing the depth of his connection to the young man standing before him. As Ezra unsheathed his glistening weapon, the sound of metal sliding against leather filled the air, resonating with unspoken promises and a shared history. His trembling hands held the sword aloft, its blade catching a glimmer of light, as if it held within it the echoes of countless battles fought and victories won.

"Joshua," Ezra whispered, his voice barely audible amidst the surge of emotions, "I want to pass down my sword to you. This sword has brought me countless victories, may it become an extension of your arm, guiding and protecting you on all the adventures that lie ahead."

Joshua stood frozen, his eyes fixed on the gleaming blade that seemed to hold the weight of Ezra's unwavering love and trust. As he reached out to accept the sword, his hand mirrored the storm of emotions swirling within him.

"Thank you," Joshua whispered, his voice quivering with a mixture of gratitude and unspoken promises. He held the sword delicately, as if cradling a fragile piece of his mentor's soul. In that moment, he knew that this symbol of legacy carried not only the weight of a weapon but also the hopes and dreams of an unbreakable bond forged through time.

Tears welled up in both their eyes. In that quiet exchange, the passing of a sword became a testament to their shared journey, unbreakable bond, mentorship, and family.

"Okay, it's time to carve your name in the wall," Ezra said. "Let's gather the class."

Joshua smiled solemnly; Ava knew this was a moment that he would never forget. Even in these uncertain times, she wanted him to find joy. Joshua grabbed Ava's hand and turned to Ezra with pleading eyes. Ezra received the message and nodded his silent approval.

Ava joined Joshua, Hathor, and the rest of her graduating friends in the school's basement. Lanterns cast a dim light across the room, causing the basement to appear older than the rest of the building. Its walls were lined with aged wood that smelled like a forest of damp trees. Forty graduates gathered, standing almost in a trance in front of a worn stone wall. Ava inched closer to the wall that seemed more like a shrine than a foundation holding up the school. Ava focused her eyes, thousands of deeply carved names started to shine in the fires' flickering light. The students wrapped their arms around one another, connecting to all the generations that had carried on this tradition. This wasn't just about friendship—over the course of their studies at the Land School, they had become a family. Finally, something clicked in Ava's mind. These were her brothers and sisters, and it was their collective duty to look after one another.

After they came out of their meditative huddle, the students took out their weapons. Joshua unsheathed his new sword and made his way to the wall. The crowd of graduates parted to let him pass. Those at the top of the class had the honor of being the first to carve their names into history. With his last stroke, Joshua rounded out the 's' of his last name: Briggs. The other students cheered. As each student wrote their name on the wall, the class grew louder and louder. Once everyone was done, the graduates returned to their huddle and jumped up and down in celebration.

Ava loved seeing them so happy, but there was a sadness there, too. After this, they faced a dangerous battle, an uncertain future. She hugged herself and tried to force the thought from her mind.

Ezra joined the celebration and entered the huddle with the students. They immediately quieted down to hear him speak.

"I just wanted to say a few words before we head to the ceremony. I am so honored to have been involved in part of your lives. You have taught me and helped me grow into a better leader, a better elder, and overall, a better person. I will never forget the kindness you have shown me and the strength you have brought to this school."

A couple of students whooped from the middle of the huddle. A huge grin spread across Ezra's face. "Now, my fellow Acathodians . . . Are you ready to go to Hadal?"

Various shouts of "Yes!" and "You bet!" echoed around the room.

"Oh, come on, you guys can do better than that. I said, are you ready?" Ezra was obviously trying to keep the spirit and joy of a graduation ceremony alive, though Ava could see deep into his eyes the pain of today's event. The class erupted into roars and hollers as they banged their weapons together. Ava could hear the pride, the rage, and the fear within their shouts.

"There it is! That's the kind of power you guys are bringing to fight our foes!"

Ezra began handing out robes and pendants that each student was to wear for the graduation ceremony. Once the students had adorned themselves in the proper garb, Ezra led them out of the basement. Ava followed them out, not saying a word. She noticed her mother standing in the lobby and went to join her.

"That was intense," she said.

"It's a great honor that you were invited. That might have been the first time someone from outside the class was allowed to attend."

Ava's jaw dropped. "Really? Wow, I had no idea."

"Joshua's a good boy. *Man*, actually." Sura smiled. "See how he's last in line? There's a reason for that. The strongest are always in the back. Like in a wolf pack, they are there to protect everyone else and make sure that no one falls behind."

Yes, he did that for me, Ava thought, thinking of the times he'd stood up for her. *Who's going to keep me from falling behind when he's gone?*

She stared down at her toes, refusing to voice her worries. She would make do. Somehow.

Sura put a comforting hand on her daughter's back. "Let's head outside to our seats so that they can finish up here."

Out on the beach, the decor was astonishing. Flower petals littered the sand in a constellation of white and gold. The long, white aisle runner was embroidered with the Land School's blue crest. Ava and her mother sat down on chairs made of beautifully carved white oak. Harper accidentally knocked one seat over as she ran to join the Greenes in the second row. Tranquil music filled the air as Lundlow, Yara, Agatha, Ezra and the other elders took their places on the wooden stage at the end of the runner.

"Here we go," Sura said.

Ava took a deep breath, trying to reconcile her joy and sadness. Soon, it was time for the graduating students to process down the aisle. There were no more tears or fear. Every student had his or her game-face on. As the last students passed by, Ava managed to catch Joshua's eye for long enough to give him an encouraging smile. He winked back at her. When the graduating class had been properly seated on stage with the elders, Agatha stood up.

"Today is a special day," she proclaimed. "Today, I get to see some of the most wonderful Acathodians take up arms to defend our people and our home. As your defense teacher, I can confidently say that our enemies have no idea what's coming to them!"

With this, the audience went wild with cheers and battle cries. The sounds echoed across the water and burst into the trees. If only their enemies could hear them now. Agatha sat down and Ezra took her place at the center of the stage. He directed his attention to the graduates behind him.

"A few minutes ago, I saw you all proudly carve your name into the stones of this school. Due to these fraught times, you are being forced to leave your home early, but I can assure you that you will never be forgotten. When you go to your new home today, remember your time here. Remember how you grew and evolved into the Acathodians that stand before me today."

Ezra paused, taking time to study the faces of each student.

"As I look upon you now, I see a multitude of different emotions. I see smiles and laughter, I see frowns and tears. I also see pride and courage, anger, and a desire for vengeance. I, too, feel these emotions. Perhaps most of all, I am angry. I am angry that we are forced to live this way, angry that we have to send our children into battle. You have so much to give this world besides your swords, axes, and knives. But, right now, we need you to be shields for those who can't defend themselves. I remain forever hopeful—"

A student in the audience stood up suddenly. In silence, the student stood frozen, looking past the stage to the water, forcing other heads to turn.

Another student screamed. After that, people began to murmur and shout. Unable to see over the bodies in front of her, Ava twisted in her chair to get a glimpse of what was out there. By then, sheer panic was sweeping through the crowd. People were jumping up, taking off, running, screaming.

Ava almost fell over her own feet as she shot up from her seat and caught sight of what was heading for them.

It was a massive wave, so high and imposing that it nearly blocked out the sun in the sky.

Students fled from the beach, trying to run back to the safety of the school. They tripped over one another and screamed as they saw the massive tsunami swell above them.

Ezra shouted for people to run. Agatha motioned people inland, running that way herself.

"Mom! What do we do?" Ava yelled in terror.

Sura scrambled between Ava and Harper and linked their arms together. "Hold on tight, girls. Don't lose sight of one another."

Harper and Ava looked at each other with wide eyes.

"You are Acathodians! You can survive this!" Sura shouted. "Dive in strong, ride the wave, and swim as fast as you can!"

The world seemed to move in slow motion. Ava's breathing grew heavy. She saw Hathor, Seal, and Mr. Blob huddled together beside Ezra and Joshua. The apex of the wave rose high above them, its shimmering blackness blocking out the sun entirely. Ava heard faint cries drowned out by the roar of the water as the wave descended upon them.

"Take care of each other!" A simple sentence spoken by Sura, full of love and strength.

Before Ava could tell her mother she loved her, the three ran into the trembling torrent, desperately trying to hold onto each other. But the wave easily broke their grasp and Ava quickly found herself spiraling alone and along the shadowy realm of the sea. Trying to keep her underwater breathing normal, Ava kicked against the current and snaked her head about desperately trying to locate anyone she could. Every so often, something caught in the current slammed against her, throwing her back. An array of darkened, twisted figures passed Ava's sight too quickly for her to recognize a face. Yet every single cry for help was impossible to avoid. The sound of screams meshed as a choir of chaos that rang through the ripples straight into Ava's heart.

As the rush of the water slowed, Ava's contorting body found balance.

A different type of scream met Ava's ears. This sound was not one of grief, it was born in fear and panic. Grindylows! What looked like fifty grindylows swiftly swam through the water, viciously attacking the helpless Acathodians.

With no way to fight back, it was a massacre. The blood-tinted water moved slowly towards Ava, as if the blood were fingers on an outstretched arm, coming to drag her to her grave. Ava swam from those red lanky fingers, and from the shrieks of those killed by the grindylows.

Still breathless and beaten from the tidal wave, she paddled, her head screaming with pain. Exhausted, just when she was thinking about giving up, hope crawled back into view. A golden sword glistened through the crimson water. Ezra's beacon of hope drew a fresh breath into Ava's depleted self. Though far away, it was what she needed to keep going. The silhouettes of other Acathodians made their way towards Ezra, too.

Ava slowed. A large brick wall stood stuck in the sand, as if it was a lost puzzle piece detached from the whole. The once admired school walls that had glistened in the sun, now lay lifeless, swallowed by the tormented waters. A thunderous impact shook Ava. Her body had no time to react, she found herself pinned against the broken wall, held by a snarling grindylow. As she stared into the grindylow's cold eyes, it smiled, baring the flesh from its last victim in its teeth. Its foul, hot breath fanned her face.

It was playing with her. Ava tried to fight back, quickly realizing she didn't have the strength to break loose. Her screams echoed in her ears. The grindylow's hot breath inched closer to her neck. Ava looked out into the dark empty water; her eyes as transparent as a window to lost hope. There was no one to save her.

Ava closed her eyes and thoughts of her mother crept into mind—laughs, smiles, her old home, her cozy chair. She pictured Joshua and Harper. Her life wasn't long, but it was full of love, and at the end of the day, that's all that mattered. Ava held her breath as the grindylow sunk his razor-sharp teeth deeply into her delicate skin. Agonizing pain shot through Ava's body. Yet just before Ava met her end, death's grasp was ripped away with a jolt. An oak chair, lost in the current, was her hero. The grindylow's head was caved-in from the impact. The grindylow's eyes were just as empty, just as cold, just as dark in death, as they were in life.

Ava could still see Ezra's golden sword, shimmering off into the distance. The golden sword called her, guiding her to safety. Ava held her neck with one hand, trying to stem the flow of blood. Her legs desperately kicked forward, inharmoniously with the other. Ava's vision was blurry, yet her ears picked up the most amazing sound: Harper's voice screaming her name. The rush of the water swept her off her path, with arms beneath her, holding her tightly.

"I am here, I got you," Harper said, her voice visibly shaken with emotion.

Ava reached her hand up, touching Harper's face. The sunlight pierced through the blue water, illuminating Harper's skin. Ava sighed in relief and slowly, the world fell away.

22

Death of a Songbird

As the water sank back into the sodden earth, Ava slowly awoke. Her body rested on the cold, wet ground, her shallow, infrequent breaths in sync with the lethargic beat of her heart. Ava reached up to feel her neck, now completely healed. Slowly, Ava rejoined reality. She tried to focus her vision as she listened to her classmates' screams. Ava sat up, looking around at the destruction. The school walls were crumbling, and a portion of the west wing had been carried a few meters away from the rest of the building. A few dozen Acathodian students were rushing around to help others who lay motionless on the ground. Some were crying over their fallen friends. Ava's voice quivered when she saw Mr. Blob holding Seal in a tight embrace as she lay limp in his arms. As Ava watched Mr. Blob's uncontrollable weeping, Ava's breath stuck in her throat, along with her unspoken words and cries.

"Mr. Blob!" Ava's hoarse voice cried out. Ava started to crawl toward Mr. Blob and her fallen friend. Maya, the girl who had already lost her mother to this war, was desperately crawling on the ghostly beach, crying out to her best friend who was sprawled on the sand, lifeless. Ava had to turn her head, it was too difficult to see Maya's pain. Closer to the shore, Carl stared into the abyss of his own thoughts, clearly in a state of shock. Ava felt someone fling themselves onto the sand near her. A warm body hugged her tightly. The embrace was painful yet comforting.

"Harper!" Ava's voice rang with joy.

The girls cried into each other's arms.

"Ava, are you okay?" Harper asked as she checked Ava's neck. "Your neck looks better, I gave you Yara's healing potion."

Ava lay still, trying to process Harper's question. Are you okay? That term meant so many things right now. Ava was alive, but very far from okay.

"I can't really move," she said, her voice still raspy.

"You just need time. The potion is still working," Harper said while helping Ava sit back up.

"Harper, are you okay? Ava asked.

"Yes, no, I don't know. I have been running around healing people, checking in on you and our friends. I know once I stop helping, stop moving, my brain will begin to process the loss and I won't be able to stop crying," Harper acknowledged.

Ava hugged Harper tightly. "So, let's start moving".

Harper didn't move. She was clearly trying to block something, hide reality. Ava slowly raised her left hand onto Harper's shoulder, ever so slightly brushing Harper to the side. Initially, Harper resisted, but then obliged Ava's need for truth.

Not far from where she lay, Ava saw a group of students gathered around Agatha's lifeless body. Agatha's vacant eyes stared upon the heavens; her skin bereft of color. A noticeable gash on her neck and ribs, still wet with her blood, added to the vermilion sand. The sight was too much to handle. Rolling flat onto her back, Ava diverted her eyes to the clear blue sky. The calmness of the birds flying gracefully over her head was surreal. For them, it was as if no tragedy had occurred. Ava could not help but think, at least Agatha had a peaceful view as she left this world.

Harper positioned herself next to Ava. They sat side by side in silence for a long moment. When silence was no longer comforting, Ava spoke. "Agatha."

"I know," Harper said softly. "Lundlow, too."

Ava had to ask, no matter how scared she was to say their names, fearful of the answer.

"My mom? Joshua?"

"Joshua, is fine, he is helping Ezra and Hathor rescue as many people as possible." Harper paused then continued, her voice soft. "I haven't seen Sura yet."

Ava couldn't help but cry. Harper reached for Ava's hand, held it tightly. Maybe it was too difficult to think of her mother resting on the white sand, held in place as her own tombstone.

"Seal," Ava whispered. "Seal is . . ."

She couldn't bring herself to finish the sentence. Harper nodded, tears streaming down her cheeks. "We lost a lot of our friends today."

Ava stood up shakily. On wobbly legs, she began to make her way back to the living. She locked eyes with Joshua from a distance and stopped. Joshua looked up to the sky with tears in his eyes and smiled. He began to walk toward Ava, eventually breaking into a run. Still catching his breath, he wrapped her up in his arms.

"Go help the others!" Ezra shouted.

Ava rushed toward the crumbling school alongside Joshua and Harper. When they arrived at the ruins, the three were stunned by the destruction. The roof where Ava and Sura had watched the sunrise was now scattered along the beach in pieces. Ava scanned the bodies that littered the ghostly grounds, but her mother wasn't anywhere to be found. As she searched, she heard a gentle cry for help.

"Logabet!" Harper and Ava ran over to their friend.

"My leg . . ." Logabet whimpered.

Ava tried to avert her eyes from the mangled wreckage below his left kneecap as they helped him off the ground.

"It's going to be okay, let's get you to Yara, I'm sure she can help you."

Seeing all the students who were alive on the beach gave Ava hope. She had a rush of energy to keep searching for her mother. Yara ran over to retrieve Logabet from Ava and Harper and set to work treating his leg. Deciding that he was safe with Yara, Ava ran back toward the school. On her way, she saw Mr. Blob looking for something on the ground.

"Mr. Blob!" Ava ran up and gave him a big hug.

"What are you looking for?" Ava asked.

"Seal always wore a bracelet, but it must have been ripped off by the wave. I need to find it for her . . ."

"Harper!" Ava yelled.

Her friend came trotting over. "What's wrong?"

"Help Blob find Seal's bracelet. I need to find my mom!"

Ava ran off, frantically searching for any sign of her mother. She screamed desperately but there was no reply. Her cries echoed over the waves, the sorrowful notes bouncing back to haunt her. The world started to spin as if she was still caught in the wave. Her breath grew quick and shallow as the hopelessness of her search began to set in. Sura was nowhere to be found. Terrified, Ava slumped over on her knees, trying to catch her breath.

"Ava!" Joshua howled. "Ava, where are you?"

Ava picked herself up off the ground and followed the sound that was traveling through the damaged trees. Ava saw Joshua racing towards her, his arms swiping away the sharp broken branches.

"I can't find my mom," Ava said, choking on her heavy sobs. "W-where is she?"

"We can look for her together. The wave could have carried her past the school. Or . . ." Joshua stopped.

"I know, she could have been dragged out to sea." Ava finished Joshua's thought. Ava couldn't say the other possibility out loud, but the image of her mother lying still, dead eyes staring into the heavens, made its way into Ava's mind, and there it would stay until they found her. Ava and Joshua walked deeper into the woods behind the school. Droplets of water with a disturbing tinge of red caught Ava's gaze. As she stared up at the crown of the trees, she jerked back with horror at the sight of deceased Acathodians dangling there, as if they were rotting fruit on a decaying tree.

"Mom!" Ava called out again. There was no reply. "Joshua—" Ava's voice trembled with fear and panic.

"Don't you dare, Ava. Your mother is a survivor."

A horn sounded from the beach.

"Something is happening," Joshua said, on high alert. "Ava, I promise we will keep looking, but we need to head back to the beach."

Ava didn't budge, her eyes wildly surveying this dystopian landscape, every image more horrifying than the last.

Joshua grabbed Ava's hand. "I promise Ava, we will find her, but we need to head to the beach."

Ava whipped her hand away from Joshua's. "No, Josh, go if you need to. I have to keep looking!"

The sound of the horn pierced the wind again.

"Ava, I understand, but that horn, that horn is telling us there is immediate trouble, we must head back."

Ava never saw Joshua so unsettled. She sighed, frustrated, but followed Joshua from out of the woods. Every step felt like a betrayal to her mother. As they arrived at the shoreline, they made eyes with an emerging Acathodian warrior, demanding all to flee into the water with him.

"Why does he need us in the water?" Joshua questioned. Joshua called out to Ezra to get his attention.

"Another wave is coming! Get in the water now!" Ezra shouted.

Ava called to her friends who were still looking for Seal's bracelet by the crumbling school building. "Harper, Mr. Blob, come quickly! Get in the water!"

Before Ava could realize what was happening, debris began to rain down on them. Ava glanced up at a giant block of the school's foundation that was about to fall onto Harper and Mr. Blob.

"Harper!" Ava shouted, her eyes bulging.

Harper threw her hands over her head. Out of nowhere, Sura rounded the corner of the school and flung herself at Ava's friends, knocking Harper and Mr. Blob out of harm's way. A cloud of dust engulfed her friends and mother.

"*Mom*!" Ava's scream shook the heavens.

As the dust started to settle, Harper could be seen planted to the sand in fear and disbelief. She was visibly stunned, staring at the large boulder that almost took her life. It was when Ava stood before them that she saw her mother under the massive rock. Sura's face and arm could be seen, her hair and skin once beautiful and glowing was now gray, painted with dust.

"Mom? Mom!" Ava tried in vain to lift the debris from her mother. "Help me . . . please!" she wailed.

Harper and Mr. Blob jumped to their feet and joined Ava. Joshua ran up to help, but it would not budge. With each futile pull, with every failed heave, her friends slowly stopped trying. It was hopeless, and too late to save Sura.

She was gone.

Ava fell to her knees, placing her hand on her mother's head. As she stroked Sura's dusty black hair, she began to hum the song of the birds, the song her mother always sang to her. She hoped the song would find her mother's ears in comfort, even though the light in her eyes was already gone. There were no last words, no final goodbyes.

Ezra slowly approached and kneeled next to Ava and wrapped an arm around her cold shell of a body.

"We need to go," Ezra said, choking back tears. He too felt the sting of Sura's death.

Too stunned, Ava did not move from her mother's side. The screams around them grew louder as the wave came closer, yet no one around Ava moved. She stared numbly, unable to feel fear. Unable to feel anything at all.

"Ava, please . . ."

Joshua sat next to the paralyzed girl and reached for her hand. Harper rested her arm on Ava's back. Ezra rose and took a step back, keeping one eye on the powerful wave.

"We have to go," Joshua whispered. "Your mother would have wanted you to be safe."

In a daze, Ava nodded. Joshua swept her up and she clung to him with everything she had. As they all ran toward the water, Ava looked back at her mother for the final time. One last silent goodbye.

The surviving Acathodians pounded into the waves and submerged themselves deep in the water. Ava swam alongside Joshua and Harper as they journeyed farther into the sea. No one spoke, no one could. The sorrow of loss overwhelmed their minds and voices. They swam for hours.

When things seemed at their darkest, a bright and wondrous light caught Ava's gaze. Before her was a sight so beautiful, so grandiose, that just for a moment it blocked all of Ava's pain.

Hadal.

Printed in the USA
CPSIA information can be obtained
at www.ICGtesting.com
LVHW041709270723
753439LV00002B/305

9 798218 145538